# MARY'S RENEWAL

*Cripple Creek Colorado Gold Series Book 1*

## ELLEN ANDERSON
## KATIE WYATT

**Royce**Cardiff
Publishing House
WHOLESOME INSPIRATIONAL ROMANCE

**Royce**Cardiff
P u b l i s h i n g   H o u s e
WHOLESOME INSPIRATIONAL ROMANCE

*Dear Reader,*

*It is our utmost pleasure and privilege to bring these wonderful stories to you. I am so very proud of our amazing team of writers and the delight they continually bring us all with their beautiful clean and wholesome tales of faith, courage, and love.*

*What is a book's lone purpose if not to be read and enjoyed? Therefore, you, dear reader, are the key to fulfilling that purpose and unlocking the treasures that lie within the pages of this book.*

**NEWSLETTER SIGN UP GET FREE BOOKS!**

***https://ellenanderson.gr8.com/***

# CONTENTS

# A PERSONAL WORD FROM AUTHORS

WE WANT TO THANK YOU FOR ALL YOUR continued support for all of our bestselling series. We wouldn't be where we are now without all your help. We can't thank you enough!

We had a lot of fun writing this series about adventures, hardships, hopes, loves, and perseverance. Writing this Historical Western Romance was a magical time.

Come and join us on this wild west romance adventure and meet the locals!

Read all the books in Cripple Creek Colorado Gold Romance Series by bestselling authors Ellen Anderson and Katie Wyatt!

Cripple Creek Colorado Gold Romance Series

We sure hope you enjoy reading it!

Ellen and Katie

# PROLOGUE

## Mary Howard

ONE MOMENT, MARY WAS BAKING BREAD FOR THAT night's supper. The next, she was opening the front door of her small house to find George Baker standing there, a look on his face that sank her heart before he even opened his mouth.

"May I come in?" George asked, holding his hat in his hands.

Mary felt like she couldn't speak. George was her husband's supervisor. Alfred looked up to George, and the two men were friends as well as coworkers.

3

Although Mary and Alfred sometimes had George and his wife Alice over for dinner or saw them at church services, George had never come to the house by himself during the day. And there was only one reason that he would be standing there.

"Just tell me," Mary said, pressing a hand to her chest to try to keep her composure. "I can't abide the social niceties, George. What happened to him?"

"He's gone," George said quietly, sorrow in his eyes and sympathy in his voice. "I'm sorry, Mary. It was a horrible accident. The blast...he was right in its line. It took him instantly. There was nothing anyone could do."

Mary closed her eyes for a moment, breathing through the grief that was washing over her. Her husband Alfred was gone. They had only been married a short five months—just at the beginning of their lives together. Now it had been cut short. Alfred, with his love for building things and his sense of humor and his sweet sensitivity...she was never going to see him again. Never talk to him again.

"Perhaps we should sit down," Mary said, feeling quite weak suddenly.

George pushed the door open further, guiding her inside without touching her. "Sit down," he urged, gesturing toward the worn blue settee that Alfred's mother had given them when they married.

Mary sat, sweeping strands of brown hair out of her face as she tried to collect her thoughts. "Nora," she said, looking around. "Nora is...she must be out in the garden."

"I'll get her," George said, quickly moving through the small house to go out the back door.

Mary used the moment she had alone to let a tear slide down her cheek. She had gotten married with so much hope for the days ahead. She had wanted to make Alfred a wonderful wife, to bear him children and to build their lives together in the small town of Bramble, Iowa. Alfred's mother and both of her parents had been at the small wedding, along with Mary's sister, Nora. Her parents and Alfred's mother had all died since the wedding, a terrible winter taking so many loved ones from them.

Now Alfred was gone as well, and Mary and Nora were all on their own. Even with Alfred's mining wages, they had been struggling to make ends meet. Mary didn't know how she and Nora would survive. She and Nora did washing and sewing for other families to bring in a little extra money, but that would never keep food on the table. Especially...

Mary placed her hand on her stomach, closing her eyes again. She had been wondering the last few days if her dream of becoming a mother was already underway. Now that little piece of joy she had been carrying with her became bittersweet, and she didn't know whether to hope that some piece of Alfred would live on in their child or hope that there was no child to bring into poverty, without a father.

"God, please help us," Mary whispered, dropping her head into her hands. "Alfred, we needed you."

Footsteps were moving toward her, and then Nora was beside her on the settee, the two sisters holding each other tightly. Mary gave in to her tears then, letting them flow down her cheeks as she cried for her poor husband and their lost future and the child that might be within her, about to enter a world without security or a father.

"I'm so sorry," Nora said, hugging Mary close. "George told me everything. Mary, I'm sorry. Your worst nightmare."

Mary picked her head up, using the sleeve of her dress to wipe at her eyes. "My worst nightmare?" she asked. Of course the death of her husband was a terrible nightmare, but there was something in Nora's tone that made Mary think that she meant something more specific.

Nora seemed to realize that George might have told her everything, but perhaps he hadn't told Mary everything. "Alfred had been drinking," Nora said quietly. "Right before the blast. George saw him pull a flask out of his boot. He thinks Alfred wasn't thinking straight."

Mary felt numb to the information, like her mind and heart couldn't process anything else right now. Mary and Alfred had only known each other a few short months before they had married. Alfred and his mother had moved to Bramble, where Mary had grown up, to be closer to Alfred's uncle after Alfred's father had passed. They had met at church and then gotten to know each other over the next few weeks while Alfred courted her.

Mary had liked Alfred, and they'd had a lot to talk about. When he had first told her about how hard it had been to lose his father and how he had been struggling, she'd felt such sympathy for him. At the time, she hadn't been able to imagine losing a parent. She had admired how much love Alfred was capable of, and she saw that love when he talked about his father.

It hadn't been until after they married that Mary had realized that Alfred had turned to drink to cope with his father's death. At first, it was just the occasional drink, and Mary tried to trust her husband and pray about it. But when his mother also passed, the drinking got much worse, and Mary knew that there was a real problem. She hadn't had any idea how to cope with that problem, and even explaining to Alfred what a toll it was taking on them financially hadn't opened his eyes to what he was doing.

Now it had taken him from this world. From her. Possibly from their unborn child.

"What are we going to do, Nora?" Mary whispered, shaking her head. "We've lost so much, and..."

Nora put her hand on Mary's stomach. Mary had confided in Nora that she thought she might be with child just a few days ago, and the two had kept the happy news to themselves. Now it was at the fore-front of both of their minds.

"We'll figure it out," Nora told her. "One way or another, Mary. We still have each other. And maybe a little one on the way."

"But if I am with child, that will make things so much harder," Mary said. She felt her hands tremble, and then tears were falling down her cheeks again. "I don't know what to do without Alfred. I know he made mistakes, but he was my husband, and he's gone. He's gone, Nora."

Nora wrapped her arms around Mary, rocking her back and forth as she cried. "God will show us a way," she said, over and over again. "He always provides."

# CHAPTER 1

## Mary Howard

AUGUST 3, 1888

MARY SAT IN HER SEAT ON THE TRAIN—THE SAME seat she had occupied for the last two days. Her head leaned against the window, and her hand rested on her swollen stomach. She was eight months along, and her baby would come in just a few short weeks. By that time, she would be settled in Cripple Creek, Colorado, her new home.

It had been Nora's idea, back in February when Mary had first learned of Alfred's death. They had talked many hours about how they were going to make ends meet now that they were on their own. When Mary got confirmation that she was with child, their talks had grown only that much more serious. At first, Mary had balked against Nora's idea of picking up their lives and moving out west to live with their friend Jessamine and help her run the boarding house she had started several years back. Both Mary and Nora had grown up in Iowa, and even though their parents had passed and there was little left to tie them to the town, it was still home.

But as the weeks had gone on and their money situation had become more and more strained, Mary had finally had to admit that Nora's solution was by far their best one. Nora wrote to Jessamine, and Jessamine had said she would love to have her dear childhood friends come out to stay with her.

So they had begun to plan. It wasn't a small project, two women selling everything and moving out west. They'd had to sell the house and the livestock and pay off Alfred's debts that Mary hadn't known existed. George and his wife had been an immense help to them, and over the past few months, Mary and Nora had stayed with George and Alice. George had offered to pay both Mary and Nora a wage if they tutored his seven children over the summer months. It had been a kind gesture, from one friend to another. Mary knew it had just been a way for George and Alice to help the two sisters put a little money in savings before they moved away. And Mary would always remember their kindness.

But now it was time to get settled in her new home before the baby arrived, and Mary had any number of emotions fighting within her. It was hard to leave everything behind, even though what she was leaving behind had been difficult and scary and uncertain. There were moments when all she felt was the hope of a new life, and moments when all she felt was regret over what she had lost in the last year.

Nora was always with her to lift her spirits in the dark times, and Mary thought that without the steady support of her sister, she might have stumbled in her faith along the way. But Nora never stumbled, and that gave Mary strength.

"Just a few minutes now," Nora said from her seat beside Mary. "Oh, how I look forward to walking about in the open air again. Just two days travel, but it really makes you remember to appreciate fresh air and long walks, doesn't it? Then again, these trains are just a modern miracle. Think of how Ma and Pa would have traveled from Iowa to Colorado when they were our age. I'm sure they would have loved to have had a train to take them on such a long trip in just two days. Thank God for progress."

Mary smiled as Nora proved just what Mary had been thinking about at the time—that Nora never faltered. She reached for her sister's hand and pressed it warmly. "I'm glad for you, Nora. Life is much easier with you by my side."

"What a dear," Nora said, covering Mary's hand with hers and smiling warmly. "We always have each other. God has always blessed us with that. And soon we will have Jessamine as well. Remember all the fun we used to have?"

Mary nodded. She did. Nora, Mary, and Jessamine had been inseparable when they were younger. Jessamine was the liveliest of the three, with Nora close behind her. Mary had often tagged along just because she didn't want to be left out. Nora and Jessamine would climb trees and skin their knees and soil their dresses and get in trouble with their mothers. Mary had always been the voice of reason, reminding them that they needed to still find time to practice their needlepoint and help bake bread.

She was responsible to a fault, but Nora and Jessamine had always done their best to liven her up. Mary was as excited to see their old friend again as

Nora was, and the moment was fast approaching as the train slowed down, puffing its way into Cripple Creek, Colorado's, station.

The whistle blew, and the train slid to a stop. People began to move around the cabins, gathering their things, and Mary looked over at Nora. The sisters exchanged smiles, Mary's holding somewhat more trepidation than Nora's. Together, they walked out of their train cabin and through the aisle. They filed down the stairs behind the other departing passengers, stepping onto the platform.

Mary barely had a moment to look around and gather her bearings before Jessamine's arms were around her, squeezing tightly.

"Mary Howard, as I live and breathe, you haven't aged a day! Motherhood has already made you radiant!" Jessamine crowed before pulling back to look at Mary, a wide smile on her face. "I couldn't be happier to see you." She put her hand on Mary's stomach, her eyes warm. "And this baby you're bringing. It fills my heart to think that we'll soon have a little one to care for."

"Jessamine," Mary said, her genuine joy at seeing her old friend so much stronger now that Jessamine was right in front of her. "You look wonderful." Mary hugged Jessamine again, Jessamine's brown curls falling from her attempt at a tidy hairstyle and brushing against Mary's face. "Thank you for taking us in. You are such a blessing."

Nora cleared her throat with playful pointedness. "Excuse me, but I am here as well."

"Nora!" Jessamine cheered, leaving Mary to wrap her arms around Nora as well. "Of course you are here, my dear friend, and I couldn't be happier about it. I have been counting down the minutes until you two arrived. I do love this little town and running my boarding house, but my heart will be grateful for female companionship."

As Nora and Jessamine talked eagerly, Mary took a moment to look around her new home. Her first impression was that the place was rather...dusty. People walked here and there on various errands, and horses clopped their way along the streets, pulling buggies behind them. The weather was dry—almost arid, like a desert—and the buggy wheels and skirts and shoes stirred the dust up off the ground and into the air.

The street that they were on was quite busy, but perhaps only because the train had just arrived, and people were greeting visitors and claiming freight.

There was a little row of shops on the far side of the street, and Mary noticed how tidy and pretty all the signs were. The general store, the feedstore, the bakery, the butcher's shop, Annie's Place, and then... the saloon.

Mary's appreciation diminished for the little row of shops that she had thought were so sweet and inviting. The sight of the saloon made her think of Alfred again and how much she had learned from the townspeople back home after Alfred had passed. Mary placed her hands on her stomach, as though protecting the tiny life within her from the knowledge that its father had been far more of a drunkard and a liar than Mary had ever realized. Alfred had apparently been quite skilled at hiding his vices from her, and the man whom she had known was not the man she had imagined. Never again would Mary be so blinded. Though she never would have wished for Alfred's death, Mary also knew that God had protected her from a marriage that surely would have only brought her sorrow in the end.

"What do you think?" Jessamine asked, breaking into Mary's musings. "It's a sweet little town, isn't it?"

"It is," Mary agreed, pushing her own feelings about the saloon out of her mind. It was hardly Cripple

Creek's fault that her husband had taken to drink, and she wouldn't hold the presence of a saloon against the town. "I just love the little row of shops across the way. I feel as though I could spend many a happy morning perusing goods there. You know, back home, we never had such luxuries."

Jessamine linked her arm through Mary's. "I knew that you would love the shops here. We'll go through them together. But for now, let's get you both home! I can't wait to show you my little place and the rooms I have set up for you."

On strict orders, Mary stood back as Nora and Jessamine loaded the luggage up into Jessamine's buggy. Several passersby smiled at her as they went about their business, and Mary got a friendly sense of the town. She smiled back at them, one hand still protectively on her stomach.

"Hello there," a woman said, stopping with her friend beside Mary. "Are you Eliza Mason?"

"No," Mary said, uncertain what would make the woman think so. "My name is Mary Howard. I've just arrived in town."

The woman looked over at her friend. "Oh, how foolish of me. Nelly told me you weren't, but I just was convinced."

The friend smiled warmly at Mary. "I'm Nelly Johnson, and this is Beth Brown. Sorry to stop you. Eliza is Peter Mason's wife. They live in the next town, and she's with child, you see."

"I just assumed," Nelly said, gesturing to Mary's swollen stomach. "We don't have any other mothers so close to birthing, so everyone has been eager for news of Eliza. Her husband, Peter, often comes to town on business, but Eliza keeps at home due to her condition."

"There's been a bit of a birthing lull for the past year," Nelly explained further. She patted her own stomach. "No complaints about that on my end. I have seven little ones of my own, all under nine years old, and I feel that I've provided my contribution to growing the town."

Beth laughed, nodding. "I feel as though I've done the same with my four. Although my husband is eager for another." She reached out and touched Mary's arm. "We have four girls, bless him. He so wants a son."

Mary smiled, appreciating the friendly spirit both women were showing her. "I'm sure that he does," Mary agreed. "Perhaps he will get his wish soon enough."

"Oh," Beth said, placing her hand on her stomach. "Perhaps, but there's no rush. Is this your first?"

"Yes," Mary said, anticipating the next question that would surely come. "My husband has passed, though."

Both Nelly and Beth gasped, covering their mouths with their hands.

"I'm so terribly sorry," Nelly murmured, her grief quite obvious. "How awful of us to be standing here talking about all of our children and our husbands. We just assumed—"

Mary held up a hand, smiling to reassure the woman. "Please. Don't feel guilty on my account. It has been many months since my husband passed. I had not even told him about the baby yet. It's a terrible loss, but it's not as raw any longer."

Jessamine walked over to Mary and the two women, her hand tucking into the crook of Mary's arm. "Beth, Nelly, how nice to see you both. I see you've met my friend, Mary."

"Oh," Beth said, something changing about her tone. "Yes. Hello, Jessamine. We were just getting acquainted with your...friend."

Mary could sense the shift in the tone of the conversation, though she had no idea why the shift had occurred. It was plainly obvious that Jessamine was defensive about both Beth and Nelly, yet Mary had found the two women to be nothing but pleasant during their brief interaction. And Beth and Nelly had immediately taken a metaphorical step back the moment that Jessamine had claimed Mary as her friend.

"I really need to be getting Mary back home," Jessamine said, her smile forced. "Please excuse us, ladies."

Jessamine ushered Mary toward the buggy and helped her in, following close behind. Mary hardly had a moment to situate herself between Nora and the pieces of luggage before the buggy was moving down the dusty street.

"Jessamine, what was all of that about?" Mary asked, quite confused. "Why did you act as though Beth and Nelly were unwelcome?"

"It's a long story," Jessamine said, smoothing down her skirts and batting the dust out of the fabric. "But it's best to stay away from those two. Were they asking you about your condition?"

"Yes," Mary said. "They thought I was someone named Eliza."

Jessamine arched one expressive eyebrow. "They both know Eliza Mason quite well. There is no chance that they mistook you for her. They just wanted the opportunity to grill you about who you were and why you were with child without seeming rude."

Taken aback, Mary frowned. "I see," she murmured, unsure what to make of the encounter now. She couldn't imagine why the two women would go out of their way to deceive her just to ask about her condition. Were they really so curious, and if they were, why not just ask her about it?

"Beth and Nelly are gossips," Jessamine continued. "They love to stir up trouble and know all the business of everyone in town. When they do know your business, they spread it like wildfire. It's best to avoid them altogether, and they usually do avoid me ever since I got my own back with them."

"What do you mean?" Nora asked.

Jessamine waved a gloved hand. "It was nothing, really. A very silly, silly little rumor that they were spreading, saying that my boarding house was mismanaged and dirty. A disgruntled miner refused to pay for his stay after claiming that eating the supper I cooked had made him ill with food poisoning. None of the others who ate that night were sick, though, and Dr. O'Toole assured the miner and me that his illness had nothing to do with food poisoning. Somehow Beth and Nelly got wind of it, and they began talking to everyone in town about how the boarding house would soon have to close due to my mismanagement."

Nora was shaking her head in disapproval. "What meanness. And for no reason whatsoever."

"When I found out they were the reason that my business had plummeted, I made a point of running into the two in town and loudly asking Beth how long it had been since she had seen her husband. She was so uncomfortable with the conversation that I was able to tell her that I didn't wish her any harm, but if she and Nelly kept spreading rumors about me, I would fight back with the truth about her own family situation."

"How long has it been since she's seen her husband?" Mary asked.

"No one has seen him for close to a year," Jessamine told them, shaking her head. "Now, I'm not a gossip, so I won't speculate as to why. I'll let you draw your own conclusions about where Mr. Brown has gone off to and why he doesn't enjoy being around his wife."

Mary took this new information in, wondering what to make of it. Mary knew that Jessamine was an honest and genuine person who never went looking for trouble. She was confident that the years the two women had spent apart had not changed that part of Jessamine's nature. So she didn't doubt what Jessamine was telling her, which meant that Nelly and Beth had directly lied to her and had done so in order to try to figure out who she was and whether she had a husband.

"Jessamine, I told them that my husband had passed," Mary said, looking over at her friend. "They didn't ask me about him, but I could tell the question was coming. Should I be worried?"

"Not a bit," Jessamine said firmly. "Whatever trouble those two try to stir up is meaningless. The town knows them for who they are by this point. Besides. You have nothing to be ashamed of. You were married, and your husband passed away, leaving you to raise your child on your own, which you will do with grace and wisdom—as you do everything else."

Nora took Mary's hand, squeezing it protectively. "What if Nelly and Beth try to spin some other story about Mary?"

"You leave those two to me," Jessamine said. "I wouldn't give them another thought. Now that they know that you're staying with me as my friends, I'm sure they'll leave you alone. I think that I've reached an understanding with those two." Jessamine gestured toward the house they were approaching. "You just focus on getting settled in your new homes and getting ready for our sweet little bundle of joy that will soon be arriving. Oh look, there is Dr. O'Toole now. I asked him to stop by this afternoon to get acquainted with you, Mary. He'll be helping with your care."

Mary looked ahead toward the house, making eye contact with the man who stood near the front door, his hat in his hands. He was a good-looking man with sandy blond hair and a chiseled jaw. His eyes, even from a distance, looked friendly.

All the same, Mary wasn't sure about him. "Jessamine, I thought I would be able to speak with a midwife."

"You will," Jessamine assured her. "But Lydia is a fair distance away. Nearly an hour. She'll be there for the birth, of course, and you'll meet her beforehand, but in the meantime, if something were to happen where you would need to see a doctor immediately, we have Dr. O'Toole on hand."

The buggy came to a stop, and Jessamine stood up, shaking out her skirts. "Come, come," she urged. "I can't wait for you to see it all!"

Mary stood as well, following Jessamine out of the buggy and into her new life and her new home.

## CHAPTER 2

## Dr. Simon O'Toole

SIMON STOOD OUTSIDE THE BOARDING HOUSE, watching the horse-drawn buggy approach with a driver and three women sitting in the back of it, luggage piled around them. Jessamine was a woman for whom he had great respect. She ran the boarding house largely on her own, and she did it well, dealing with all of the many difficulties that arose when one's lodgers were predominantly men working in the local mines or passing through on other work. Jessamine's spirit was not easily dampened, and her character not readily impugned. She was a hardworking woman of faith and grace, and that was why Simon did not mind taking the afternoon away from his practice in the heart of town to pay a visit to Jessamine's newly arrived and expecting friend.

The buggy pulled up to the house and stopped, and the driver quickly got down to begin helping with the luggage. Simon hurried forward to offer his own assistance as well, and he caught sight of the two new women who were making their way down from the buggy.

Both were lovely women who looked surprisingly well put together after what Simon understood had been a long journey. They looked very much like the sisters they were, both with similarly slight builds and chestnut brown hair. However, the one who was with child caught his eye in particular. There was a resilience to her expression and a quiet strength in the way she carried herself. Jessamine and the other new arrival clearly wanted to help the expectant woman, but she climbed down easily on her own, her hand on her stomach as she set foot on the ground and took a deep breath and looked around her.

She was lovely, there was no doubt. Sweet features with wide eyes framed by thick lashes and expressive eyebrows. Her lips and cheeks were pink with healthy color, and her hair shone in the sunlight.

Simon approached her, willing himself to dwell less on her pleasing appearance, given the fact that she was about to be his patient. "I'm Dr. Simon O'Toole," he said, taking the hand she extended and inclining his head over it. "You must be Mary Howard."

"Yes," she said simply. "It's a pleasure to meet you, Dr. O'Toole. Thank you for coming out to meet us."

"Hello, Simon," Jessamine said, walking up to them. "Mary's had quite a long trip. Do you mind walking her inside? I've set up the eastern sitting room to be a temporary examination room for you."

Simon extended his arm to Mary. "Of course, Jessamine. Miss Howard, if I may?"

Mary took his arm, looking back at her friend with what appeared to be just a hint of disapproval, as though she didn't like all the fuss being made over her. But Jessamine, as was her way, simply waggled her fingers with cheerful disregard for Mary's consternation.

Simon took Mary inside the boarding house, holding the door open for her and allowing her to walk first into the hallway.

"Jessamine has done quite well for herself here," Simon said, by way of making conversation with his patient. "This is as welcoming a boarding house as I've ever seen in my travels, and it's really all down to Jessamine's efforts."

Mary was looking around the place, spinning in a slow circle as she took in the wooden floors and the soft woven rug that led down the hallway. To the left of the hall was a room filled with settees and armchairs framed around the fireplace. Paintings hung on the walls, bringing landscapes and still-life images into the room to add warmth. Curtains hung from the windows, and there was a piano in the corner, waiting for someone to sit down and tickle its keys. Shelves filled with books called out for guests to spend an evening reading by the light of the oil lamp while the fire warmed them.

Already, Mary was halfway into the sitting room, looking about her as though she had forgotten that Simon was standing there. He smiled at her enthrallment with the place and very politely cleared his throat to draw her attention back to him.

"Oh, my apologies," Mary said, her cheeks turning a little rosier. "I was just swept away by the room's mood. If the rest of the place is like this, Jessamine has done quite well indeed."

"It is, and she has," Simon assured her. "This is the western sitting room, though, and we must cross over to the eastern one to see what Jessamine has in store for us there."

Mary followed after him, taking his arm again when he offered it. As they walked, they passed several of the young girls that Jessamine had hired to help keep the place clean, and Simon greeted them, noticing their interested surveying of Mary. Everyone would be talking about Mary and her sister for some time, even if Mary hadn't arrived with child. Cripple Creek was the kind of town that loved to have new people arrive—especially women, considering there were far fewer women than men. For the most part, the curiosity would be benign and friendly, in Simon's experience.

He ushered her into the eastern sitting room, which was much smaller than the western sitting room. This one was meant to hold only a couple of people at a time, and there were only three chairs, a small card table beneath the one window, and a bookshelf beside the fireplace.

Simon closed the door behind them but left it ajar for propriety's sake. He was a doctor and was often alone with patients, but he was always quite cognizant of making a female patient feel comfortable—especially one who was new to town and had no idea who he was.

"Please, make yourself comfortable," Simon told Mary, gesturing to the chairs. "Anywhere you like. I'd like to get acquainted with you before I conduct a routine examination."

Mary sat in the faded blue chair furthest to the left in the room, her hands folded and resting on her skirts as she looked up at him, following his lead.

"I'm sure you're quite tired," he said, sitting in the chair furthest from her. "How was your journey?"

"It was much easier than expected," Mary told him. "It was long, of course, and I certainly am tired, but Nora and I were blessed with a safe journey."

He gestured toward her stomach. "Any concerns with your condition?"

"Not at all," she said, resting her hand on top of the swell her stomach. "I can feel the baby move in his usual patterns, and while I am tired and have pain at my back, I am doing well."

"That's good," Simon agreed. "You believe it is a boy, then?"

Mary smiled and lifted a shoulder. "That's up to God, of course. But I have thought of him as a boy, yes. His father would have wanted a little boy."

This was where things got a little trickier for Simon. Jessamine had told him that Mary had been married and that her husband had died, but Jessamine hadn't offered him any other information and he hadn't asked. He didn't even know how recent her loss was, and he hesitated to ask too many questions in order to avoid bringing up the grief that Mary was surely still facing. It was a terrible thing for a young woman to lose her husband under any circumstances, but especially when she was with child. Mary's life would be forever changed by this, and she was lucky that she had a friend like Jessamine who had the means to offer her a place to stay.

But if Simon's past experiences had taught him anything, it was that few women were able to stay unmarried long. There were plenty of men in Cripple Creek who were tired of being alone and would be interested in a wife. Given how few women were in Cripple Creek, the fact that Mary came with an infant would hardly be an issue. Mary might find herself with any number of proposals soon, and she would likely accept one. It would be the best thing for her in the long run, though her heart might not be ready for it yet.

If Simon was looking for a wife, he could certainly do worse than Mary Howard. But he wasn't, and he didn't plan to ever be looking for a wife. A man in his profession and in his position had no business bringing other people into his life and his home—especially someone who had already lost a husband.

"Let's examine you quickly," Simon said to Mary, standing again. "The sooner I check your vitals, the quicker you can get some rest, which will make Jessamine happy. And the world is a better place when Jessamine is happy."

Mary smiled, seeming more at ease with him. Simon had a good bedside manner—at least, that's what he had always been told. He kept up idle chitchat with Mary as he checked her heart rate and her breathing. She told him that Nora, the woman she had arrived with, was her sister, and that both of them would be staying long term at the boarding house, providing help to Jessamine in exchange for the place to stay.

"I'm afraid that there won't be enough for me to do around here," Mary said, as Simon held his fingers against the pulse in her wrist, counting. "Jessamine is such a hard worker, and Nora is as well. I know that she and Nora will do a wonderful job of running the place, and by the time I recover from birth and am ready to start pulling my weight, there may not be as much of a need for me."

"There's always work around these parts," Simon assured her. He was thinking more about the fact that her heart rate was elevated beyond where he wanted it to be. True, she had just finished a long journey, and she clearly needed rest, but he still didn't think that fully accounted for her heart rate. "Mary, if you'll just breathe in and out for me," he said, placing his hand at her neck, where her heartbeat would be more readily apparent. "Nice and slow. Try to relax into it if you can."

She did as he asked, closing her eyes as she breathed in and out in a slow, steady rhythm. Her pulse was strong, but still fast. Simon noted that the rosy color he had admired in her cheeks might not be normal for her. She could very well be flushed.

Stepping back and dropping his hand, Simon contemplated what he should do. The last thing that he wanted to do was alarm an expecting woman when it could very well be that her elevated heart rate and possibly flushed cheeks were just the result of a long trip and new surroundings. But he also knew that childbirth could be a very risky event for many women, and he didn't want to take any chances.

"Mary, I'd like to prescribe a day of bed rest," he said, striking what he hoped was a middle ground. "I'll come back by tomorrow and check on you again, just to make sure that you've settled in and the trip hasn't had any impact on the baby."

"Is there a problem?" Mary asked, looking up at him with wide eyes.

He shook his head, smiling to reassure her. "No," he said honestly. "Not at all. I'm just being extra cautious because you're a new patient and in your eighth month. A long trip can take its toll, and I want to make sure that I see you tomorrow. Your heart rate is slightly elevated, but that's easily explained by the stress of a new environment."

Mary stood, her hand on her stomach protectively. "All right. I'll go now, then. If you think that's best."

"Just for a day," he assured her again. "For safety's sake."

"Oh," Mary said, touching her hand to her head. Her other hand reached out to grip the back of the chair.

Quickly, Simon moved to her side, taking her elbow in his hand to keep her upright. "Are you faint?"

"A bit," she murmured. "It hit me suddenly."

"You're exhausted," he told her. "Adrenaline might have kept you from realizing it until now, but I think we should get you to bed quite quickly."

"Is the baby all right?"

"I'm sure it is," Simon assured her. "But I'll listen to its heartbeat as well as soon as we have you lying down." He turned, calling for help. "Jessamine?"

A young girl—part of the cleaning staff—put her head in the door instead. "Yes, Doctor? Miss Jessamine is with the new boarder at the moment."

"I need a bed for Miss Howard," Simon told her. "Is there one made up for her?"

"Yes, Doctor. Right this way."

"Can you walk?" Simon asked Mary, surveying her face for the real answer, which he wasn't assured she would actually give him.

She nodded, as expected. "Yes. The faintness has passed for the moment."

Even still, he kept his hand on her arm as he walked with her from the room and down the hall after the cleaning girl. They turned down a hallway, and then they stopped outside a door that was cracked open.

"This room is for you, Miss Howard," the girl said. "The bed is turned down."

"Thank you," Mary murmured, glancing up at Simon uncertainly.

He understood her trepidation, and he turned to the cleaning girl. "Please, tell me your name again?"

"Cynthia," the girl said. "Cynthia Hall."

"Miss Hall, would you mind staying in the room with Miss Howard and myself while I see to her?"

Cynthia nodded, eager to help. "Yes, of course, Doctor. Anything I can do."

With Cynthia's chaperoning presence, Mary stepped into what would be her new bedroom. She lay down on the bed without so much as taking off her shoes, her head resting on the pillows and her hands placed on either side of her stomach.

Simon always carried his medical supplies in a satchel that he slung across his back, and he removed that now, taking out the stethoscope that would let him listen to the baby's heartbeat. Pulling out the stethoscope, he walked over to Mary and placed it against her stomach, watching her face as she watched his movements.

The baby's heartbeat was faint but steady. He listened to it for some time, then he dropped the stethoscope and gave Mary a reassuring smile. "Your child's heartbeat sounds steady and healthy. There's nothing to worry about. You've simply overexerted yourself and need to get some rest. And preferably some food."

Mary visibly relaxed. "So he's all right?"

"He sounds exactly as I would want him to sound," Simon said, reassuring her again. Her motherly instincts had already kicked in strong, he could tell, and she had likely felt faint from the added stress of worrying about the health of her child on top of her exhaustion. He would have to be careful not to alarm her in the future in case it gave her another fainting spell.

Jessamine knocked at the door and stepped inside. "Mary, here you are. Dr. O'Toole, is everything all right?"

"Perfectly," Simon assured Jessamine. "Miss Howard is simply tired and needs to rest after a long journey.

I've just checked the baby's heartbeat and it is normal. Mary's, on the other hand, is slightly elevated, and so I'll come back tomorrow just to make sure that the bed rest has done its job."

"I won't let her lift a finger," Jessamine promised, walking over to Mary and taking her hand. "We'll get some soup brought in, and then it's a nice long nap for you, dear." Jessamine turned to look over her shoulder at Cynthia. "Cynthia, love, would you help Mary get settled in and more comfortable here while I get her soup and talk to Dr. O'Toole?"

Cynthia dropped a curtsey. "Yes, ma'am."

"Don't be so formal," Jessamine chided the girl with a shake of her head. "You know better."

"Yes, ma'am," Cynthia said, curtseying again.

Simon hid his smile as Jessamine clucked her tongue at the girl and then walked back over toward him. "Doctor, if you have a moment?"

"Certainly," Simon agreed. He looked over at Mary. "Miss Howard, it was a pleasure to meet you. I'll see you in the morning to make sure you're feeling better."

"Thank you, Dr. O'Toole," Mary said, her smile tired but sweet. "I appreciate you coming out."

Simon followed Jessamine out into the hall and then down the hall to the boarding house kitchen. It was midafternoon, which meant that most of the boarders were still out at work, so the place was empty and quiet—until Jessamine began rattling dishes around to put together a lunch for Mary.

"Nelly Johnson and Beth Brown came up to Mary in town," Jessamine told him. "As I was picking up Mary and Nora from the train station. They were trying to get the details on Mary's condition, like the busybodies they are."

Simon was unimpressed, leaning up against the wall of the kitchen, his satchel slung over his shoulder. "What does it matter?"

"It matters because those two are always up to no good," Jessamine insisted, ladling leftover stew onto a plate in a generous portion. "Mary has led a relatively sheltered life back in Iowa. The town that she was born in and grew up in—they all knew her and her sister and her family. No one has ever questioned her reputation or her family. From what I could tell from Nora's letters, Mary married the first man who courted her, and her sweet, innocent spirit kept her from seeing the worst of him until after he died, God rest his soul. She isn't made for this life out here."

"And what is this life out here?" Simon asked curiously as he took in this additional information about Mary Howard. It made her that much more interesting.

"Life in Cripple Creek is just different," Jessamine said, placing thick slices of bread on the plate beside the stew before placing it all over the fire to warm. "You have to have thicker skin. People are going to assume things about you. Question you. There are people here who, frankly, are not always nice. And I know Nelly and Beth. They'll be spreading rumors as fast as they can that Mary was never married at all and that she's been sent here by a family ashamed of her for having a child out of wedlock."

Simon didn't like the thought of that any more than Jessamine did, but he was less certain that was the inevitable outcome of Nelly and Beth having a conversation with Mary. "Let's not invite trouble," he suggested to Jessamine. "If that comes about, I'm sure that Mary will handle it and that you will help her. And of course, I'm always happy to assist in whatever way I can. Ultimately, though, rumors are just rumors. They might flare, but they quickly die when there is no truth to them."

"That's all fine and well, but I won't have my friend's reputation tarnished even for a moment," Jessamine informed him, pointing with the fork in her hand. "You have a very good reputation in this town, Doctor. People take your word for things. Can I count on you to be prepared to vouch for Mary?"

"I have no reason to doubt Mary's story or that she was married and her husband died," Simon said. "There's no medical basis for me to hang that opinion on, Jessamine. You know that."

"Yes, I do know that," Jessamine agreed. "But all the same. If you vouch for her, it will be meaningful."

Simon pushed away from the wall, straightening. He lifted a hand to rub the back of his neck, which was sunburned from the heat of the summer sun. "I think you're overthinking this. Don't go looking for trouble before it finds you."

"This is why I would never marry you," Jess informed him, taking the plate off the fire with a gloved hand. "You're too levelheaded."

"And I didn't ask you," Simon said with a chuckle. "We both know you're not looking to settle down anyway. You have your hands full here, and you didn't need a husband to make it happen, did you?"

Jessamine shook her head. "No, I certainly did not. You might be the only other person in this town as determined as I am to not get married."

"Some of us just aren't cut out for it," Simon said. "I've got to get back to the practice. I'll see you tomorrow morning. Make sure Mary stays off her feet for the rest of the day and until I see her again."

"Thanks for coming out, Simon," Jessamine said, following him out of the kitchen as she headed toward Mary's room with the plate of stew. "I love these girls. I appreciate you looking out for them."

He grabbed his hat from beside the door and tipped it at Jessamine. "That's my job."

As Simon headed back out into the midday heat, he thought about what Jessamine had said. He and Jessamine had almost a sibling sort of relationship. He admired Jessamine's determination and strength, and she relied on him as a safe and trustworthy source of advice and help. It was a mutually beneficial relationship that Simon placed a high value on. Jessamine had worked hard when she had first moved to Cripple Creek, getting the boarding house up and running. He had asked her once if she didn't plan to marry, even if just to secure help around the boarding house and provide a measure of safety for herself.

It was then that he'd realized that he and Jessamine had a lot in common—namely that neither of them were well suited for marriage. Jessamine was determined that no one would ever make decisions for her again, like she had seen her father make decisions for her mother her whole life, making Jessamine's mother miserable. Simon had a more direct personal failing than that, though.

Marriage meant having a family. A woman naturally wanted to bear children, and Simon knew that he was incapable due to a childhood injury. And so, he would never marry. He had long ago resigned himself to the single life, and most of the time, he was perfectly fine with that. His work was his passion, and his community was his family—and that would be enough.

Simon had never told Jessamine why he was determined not to get married. Only that he had no intention of taking a wife. He was sure she had questions, but she never asked them, and he had no plans to discuss it with her. Some things were personal struggles, and this was one of his.

As he walked the short distance between the boarding house and the heart of town, he thought back to Mary Howard. It brought a smile to his face for some reason, and he didn't question it. She was certainly a special woman, whether she knew it or not. There was just something about her that was calming. Something that drew him in. It didn't hurt that she was more than lovely with those wide blue eyes and chestnut hair that looked like it would waterfall down her back if loosened from its hold.

Simon shook his head, laughing to himself as he unlocked the door to his practice. Imagine if Mary Howard knew that her doctor was imagining her thick hair falling down her back. What would she think of him?

She would think him a fool, no doubt, and he would have earned the title.

"Back to business," he told himself, sitting down at his desk to look at his medical charts. "Mary Howard is just another patient."

# CHAPTER 3

Mary Howard

AUGUST 4, 1888

AS IT TURNED OUT, THE TRIP HAD TAKEN A GREAT deal out of Mary—far more than she had realized the day before. But the morning after she and Nora arrived in Cripple Creek, Mary could tell that she had been exhausted the previous afternoon because of how refreshed she felt after a long day's rest and a long night's sleep.

Now, as the sun rose higher and higher in the sky, Mary sat in the western sitting room with all of its decorative chairs and inviting paintings, watching out the window for Dr. O'Toole's arrival. She had promised Jessamine that she would do nothing until he arrived to clear her for normal activities, but she was finding it hard to wait. She wanted to go walk into the town with Nora and see this new place that she and her sister called home. All of it was so different to her, and she wanted to experience it all and get some fresh air while she was at it.

"Mary," Jessamine said, walking into the sitting room. "Are you sure I can't get you some tea?"

"No, Jess, but thank you," Mary said, smiling at her friend. "You've done plenty by making me breakfast. Don't let me interfere with your work. If I can't be a help, at least don't let me be a burden."

"You could never be a burden," Jessamine insisted.

Nora stepped up behind Jess, then walked into the room and took a seat in one of the many other chairs. "That's very true," Nora agreed, giving Mary a look. "Now stop worrying your head over being a burden. You are with child, Mary, my dear sister, and it is our job to care for you so that we have the pure joy of bouncing your sweet baby on our knees whenever you give us the chance."

Mary chuckled and shook her head. "I know that I was nervous about coming out here, but I must say that it was clearly the right decision. I feel so much lighter knowing that we are here with you, Jessamine."

"I'm so glad you're both here," Jessamine told her. "Now, I'm fixing you tea, whether you like it or not. I'm sure that Simon will be here any minute, so I'll make a cup for him as well."

As Jessamine hurried off, refusing to be deterred, Nora sat with Mary.

"How are you, dear?" Nora asked. "Truly."

"I'm much better," Mary told her. "You shouldn't worry. The baby and I are quite well and itching to be set free as soon as the doctor arrives."

"The doctor was a very handsome man, wasn't he?" Nora asked, crossing her legs and smoothing her skirts over her knees.

"Was he?" Mary asked, though she knew the answer. She had been quite aware of just how handsome Dr. O'Toole was, which had made her uncomfortable. So uncomfortable that it possibly raised her heart rate and caused her to feel flushed. She just wasn't used to being around a man she didn't know. She had grown up in the same town with people who she had known all her life. They were friends of the family or like actual family—stand-in brothers, uncles, cousins, and nephews.

Dr. O'Toole, with his shock of sandy-blond hair and his kind eyes and his broad shoulders, had made her feel the kind of flutter that she had only ever seen referenced in the romance books she had used to sneak when she was just a teenager. She had never felt that flutter about Alfred, and she had assumed that it was a thing of fiction—that the love between a man and a woman was a practical, wholesome thing that consisted entirely of affection for each other and a commitment to being lifelong partners. And it was all of those things, of course, but perhaps there was also —at least sometimes—a fluttering element as well. The kind that made your skin tingle when the person was nearby.

It wasn't that she fancied herself in love with Dr. O'Toole. Hardly! She didn't even know the man. She didn't know whether he was a man of faith with good character and a kind heart, all of which were essential traits for a husband to have. And she didn't even want to marry again, so even if he had all of those traits, she was not looking for a man to step into her life and take that husband role again.

Nevertheless. It was quite nice to know that the flutter was real and that a woman could have that sort of emotional reaction to a man, even if she had no intention of ever letting on to anyone that she'd felt the flutter when he had touched her.

"Mary," Nora said. "You didn't answer me."

"Didn't I?" Mary asked, with no intention of providing her sister with any answer at all. Luckily, she didn't have to. She pointed out the window to where she could see the doctor walking up to the house. "Dr. O'Toole is here. Nora, won't you greet him and bring him inside?"

Nora hurried to her feet, her question forgotten, and Mary leaned back in the chair, taking a slow, steady breath. She did not intend to spend any more time on bed rest, especially if it was just because the doctor set her nerves to fluttering rather than any true medical condition other than being tired after a long trip.

The door opened, and Mary could hear Nora and Dr. O'Toole conversing. Their voices grew louder as they came closer, and then Dr. Toole was in the room, smiling that warm smile as though he was genuinely glad to see her. He was every bit as handsome as he had been the day before, that chiseled jaw and those deep eyes setting him apart. Mary couldn't help but smile back at him, and as he came closer to her, she felt her heart rate pick up again, much to her chagrin.

"Good morning, Miss Howard," Dr. O'Toole said. "How are you feeling today?"

He had called her Mary the day before, but apparently he'd thought better of it and now addressed her more formally. Mary quickly set that right. "Please, Dr. O'Toole, call me Mary. And I'm much better, thank you."

"Then you must call me Simon as well," he said, pulling a seat closer to her and sitting down, setting his medicine bag on the floor. "You look refreshed today. That's excellent. I hope you got some much-needed rest."

"I did, thank you," Mary said, even as her heart rate grew steadily quicker due to his nearness. Out of the corner of her eye, she saw Nora slip out of the room, leaving her alone with the doctor.

"May I?" he asked, reaching for her wrist so that he could take her pulse like the day before.

She offered her wrist to him and his warm, rough hand wrapped around it, his fingers pressing firmly against the pulse in her wrist. There was such steady confidence in his hand. It settled Mary, almost like he could pass his confidence onto her through just a touch.

"Better," he said, nodding with approval as he counted her heartbeats. "Yes, much better. You've been resting, clearly."

She had been, but it didn't hurt that she had also had time to settle her reaction to him so that it didn't come across quite so clearly.

"Here we go," Jessamine said, coming into the room with a tray that she set on the center table. "Tea for everyone. Simon, I heard from the other room that our expectant mother is feeling better this morning."

"Much," Simon agreed, accepting a cup of tea and taking a seat as he sipped on it. "Thank you, Jessamine, but I really can't stay more than a few minutes. I have quite a few people to see to this afternoon."

Mary decided that it was now or never if she wanted to ask the doctor about the question that had been spinning around in her mind for many months now. "Doctor," she said, drawing his attention back to her. "Is alcoholism hereditary?"

He seemed taken aback by her question, and Mary didn't blame him. There were plenty of questions he might expect from her about the birthing process and even the baby's health in the first few months, but Mary was leaving that in the hands of the midwife. Neither were things she wanted to discuss with Simon O'Toole. However, she felt that he was more equipped to answer the most important question of all—was her child bound to suffer the same addictions as its father? Was it possible that Alfred's demons would continue to haunt her family?

"Well," Simon said, clearly searching for his bearings as he considered his answer. "The best that I can tell you is...it depends. There's some evidence that suggests that an addictive nature is genetic. Some people are more prone to relying on substances than others are. But, also, no. Just because there is alcoholism in a family does not mean that the children that family produces will be alcoholics. How a child is raised makes all the difference. When a child is taught to turn to faith and family and inner strength rather than to drink, whatever genetic tendencies the child might have may very well be mitigated."

Mary let out the breath she had been holding, a sense of relief washing over her. She hadn't even expressed to Nora how concerned she was that her child would carry on his father's misdeeds, so to now hear a doctor offer her some reassurance was a weight off her shoulders.

"Thank you," Mary said, adding nothing more even though it was quite obvious that Simon hoped for some explanation of her question. She wasn't ready to talk about Alfred or the complicated feelings she had about his death, and certainly not with a man who had the effect on her that Simon did. Instead, she turned the conversation to him. "Dr. O'Toole— Simon, rather," she corrected herself when he tilted his head in gentle rebuke. "I'm afraid that in the flurry of activity yesterday and my exhaustion, I failed to ask you anything about yourself. Please, since you have been so kind as to come out and look after me, tell me a bit about you."

Simon sipped at his tea and nodded. "Certainly. As you may have guessed from my name, my background is Irish, although my family are not recent immigrants. It was my grandfather who came over when he was just a lad, and my family settled in Boston for two generations. I was born out in Boston, in fact, but my father moved us out west when I was young. My grandparents had both passed, and my parents wanted to start a new life, away from the crowded streets and foul smell in the city."

"What a bold move," Mary said. "Starting over completely, and with a young child."

"Here you are, though, doing a similar thing," Simon pointed out, gesturing to her. "That's no less brave, is it?"

"I didn't have a choice," she reminded him, sipping at her tea. "My sister Nora was far braver about it than I was. It took me quite some time to adjust to the idea of moving out west."

"And now that you're here?"

"I'm eager to look around," Mary admitted. "I'm feeling better about the choice all the time. But we're talking about me again when I wanted to hear more about you. So, you moved out west, and your father took up a new business?"

Simon nodded. "Ranching. It was a new trade for him, but he was a smart man and a fast learner. He was successful in no time."

"You talk about him in the past tense," Mary pointed out, hoping that she wasn't treading on sensitive feelings.

"Yes," Simon said. "My father passed over ten years ago now. It was an accident on the ranch, actually. He was out in the pasture, and there was nearby gunfire that spooked his horse and the cattle at the same time. My father was taken off guard, thrown from his horse, and trampled by the cattle."

Mary pressed a hand to her chest, genuinely distressed. "How terrible. I'm so sorry. I should never have brought it up."

"Don't apologize," he assured her, setting his own tea down and leaning forward in his chair so that his elbows rested against his knees. "It was a tragedy, of course, but it's been some time, and I've found a way to look back on his life with happiness rather than sorrow."

Mary wondered what might have been different if Alfred had been able to do the same with the loss of his parents. The death of a father was always a tragic event, of course, but Alfred had never recovered, and he had turned to drink to soothe the ache that he felt within. Simon, on the other hand, seemed to have channeled the grief he felt into far more productive avenues.

"And your mother?" Mary asked, wondering if she was stepping into another sensitive area.

"She passed last year," Simon said, his words tinged with much fresher sorrow as he looked down at the carpet for a moment. "She was very ill, and I like to believe that her passing was a blessing to her and that she is in heaven, feeling like her old self again. But I must confess that I do miss her."

"I'm sorry to bring up such sad things," Mary said. "It's none of my business."

Again, Simon brushed off her apologies. "Please, don't be. I think it's nice to get to know a little bit about my patients and for them to know about me. I love what I do, and a lot of how I do my work is in my father's memory. He would have loved that I trained to become a doctor. I think if he had been born in other circumstances, he might have done the same."

"I'm sure he's proud," Mary murmured, even as she recognized that this conversation with Simon was doing nothing to quell the butterflies that he produced in her—the ones she very much wished not to have. Although she knew that Jessamine and Nora were both nearby, it felt as though she and Simon were the only ones in this moment, discussing the griefs of their past as they sipped their morning tea. It almost made her want to tell him about Alfred and her fears for her child, but before she could decide if she wanted to confide in him, Simon stood up.

"I really should perform a more thorough examination," he said, reaching for his bag. "And then I'm afraid I have other patients to see to. Otherwise I would be glad to stay and hear more about Jessamine's childhood friends."

Mary smiled, though she was both glad and disappointed that he was rushing off. It was really the much wiser thing to do to keep her distance from Simon, given how drawn she was to him and her disinterest in ever taking another husband. What was the point, after all, in entertaining her interest in him if she had no plans to follow through with it, even if he should ever ask to court her?

Which, of course, he was not likely to do. A man like Simon O'Toole, handsome and successful and kind, could surely land any wife that he wanted without having to settle for a woman eight months along with another man's child. His interest in her was merely politeness and good bedside manner. Nothing more. She would be wise to remember that and not fancy herself rejecting advances that had never been made in the first place.

Simon did a quick, efficient, and thorough examination, listening to her breathing, her heart, and checking her vitals. He also listened to the baby's heartbeat again, and he appeared satisfied with it and everything else.

"Very good," Simon pronounced, stepping back from her. "I think you are fully recovered from your trip, and while I recommend that you take it easy over the next few weeks until the birth, I hereby release you from bed rest."

"Thank you," Mary said, getting to her feet, her hand resting on the side of her stomach. The other hand, she offered to Simon. "I really appreciate everything you've done."

He took her hand and bowed his head over the top of it. "My pleasure, Mary." Releasing her hand, he stepped back and gathered his things into his bag. "Please give Jessamine and your sister my regards. I cannot wait for them to return before rushing off. But I hope to see you all soon enough. Perhaps you'll join us for Sunday service?"

"Yes, I hope to," Mary agreed. "I very much look forward to it. What a wonderful way to meet everyone in town."

Simon was heading toward the front door, but he stopped and looked back at her. "By the way, Mary, Jessamine tells me that you had a run-in with Nelly Johnson and Beth."

"Yes," Mary agreed, although the encounter had largely slipped her mind in the aftermath of arriving at the boarding house and being put on temporary bed rest. "I met them down at the station."

"It's best, perhaps, not to be as open with them in your conversations," Simon warned her. "I make no judgments about their intentions, but it's possible that things told to them can get easily twisted."

Mary nodded. "Yes. I'll certainly remember that."

He smiled at her, and the smile reached all the way to his eyes, making them appear even warmer. "Good. God bless, Mary, and I'll see you again soon."

As soon as he had gone, Jessamine reappeared.

"Well?" Jessamine asked. "Do you like him?"

"Of course," Mary said, reaching down for her tea so that she could distract herself with sipping it. "He's a very nice man. And a good doctor. It's nice of him to travel out here to see me."

Nora appeared in the doorway of the sitting room as well, an impish look on her face. "I think he likes you, Mary!"

Mary flushed and rolled her eyes at her sister. "Nora, please. He was entirely proper during both visits, without a hint of such things. You're imagining things." But, inwardly, Nora's words pleased her more than she cared to admit, and she could only hope that her cheeks weren't flushing.

"Simon is a confirmed bachelor," Jessamine said, walking further into the room. "But I've never known why. I've always been curious but haven't dared to ask. Perhaps you might sway him..."

"If he hasn't pursued you, then surely he has no intention of pursuing anyone," Mary said. "Why would he go all this time without making himself known to you, Jessamine, if he intended to take a wife?"

"Oh, Simon doesn't feel that way for me," Jessamine said, waving a hand as though the suggestion was foolish. "Nor I for him, for that matter. No, there's something else that holds him back—that makes him determined not to consider marriage." Jessamine shook her head. "I don't know what it is, but oh how I wish I did. That man has a secret, though. I'll tell you that much for certain."

Jessamine's words didn't sit well with Mary. She didn't like the idea that Simon was hiding something, even though she had no right to claim his transparency, given that they hardly knew each other and he was just her doctor. Still, she wanted to believe he was being open and genuine. What sort of secret might he have? It was certainly odd that a man like him wasn't already married, but then again, there was probably not an abundance of options in Cripple Creek. Was it possible that Jessamine simply was not Simon's type, and that was why he had never pursued her? Or did he have some secret reason for not taking a wife?

"Let's go out," Mary said, abruptly halting the direction of her thoughts. She needed to think about something other than Simon O'Toole. "I'm fit to be walking around, and we are going to need things for the baby sooner rather than later. How about we walk to those shops? If we find some lovely ivory fabric, I can sew some clothes for the baby."

"I'll get our things!" Nora said with enough eagerness to bring a halt to the discussion of Simon O'Toole. "I'm just dying to see the town! Let's go!"

Mary smiled. She, too, was excited to explore their new home, and she couldn't imagine two women with whom she would rather do it.

# CHAPTER 4

Simon O'Toole

AUGUST 6, 1888

"SIMON. GOOD MORNING."

Simon turned toward the sound of the voice behind him, pleasantly surprised to see Mary Howard standing on the sidewalk with fabric draped over her arm. She looked radiant, the sunlight illuminating her dark hair and pinkening her cheeks. He looked around, assuming that she wasn't walking in town by herself. Just weeks away from delivery, it was hardly a good idea for her to be out on her own.

"Hello," he said, smiling as he stepped toward her. "How are you this morning?"

Her eyes flicked behind him, and Simon turned his head to follow her gaze, noting that it rested on the saloon that he had just walked out of. He supposed that it was rather unusual for a man to be walking out of a saloon before midday, but he felt no need to explain himself in the moment. Nor did Mary ask him what he had been doing, even though her gaze seemed momentarily troubled.

"I am well," she said, refocusing on his question. "And yourself?"

"Quite well," he said. "I hope you are not shopping alone today."

Mary placed her hand on the fabric draped over her arm. "I am, actually. Nora and Jessamine and I walked the town the day before last, after you cleared me for activity, but I couldn't decide which fabrics to purchase. After some more thought, I was ready to come back into town and make my selection. But I'm afraid Jessamine and Nora were quite busy at the boarding house this morning. Apparently, there was an influx of workers for the new steel mill."

"Indeed there was," Simon agreed. "Unfortunately that means I may be on call more than usual. New workers in a mill spell trouble, I'm afraid." He straightened his hat and gave her an apologetic smile. "I shouldn't talk of such things, though. Forgive me. Are you through with your shopping?"

"I am," Mary said. Her eyes once more flickered to the saloon behind him. "I'm just making my way home."

He wondered if she was looking at the saloon because she was hungry. It was nearly high noon, and in her condition, she needed to replenish herself after a morning of walking.

"You didn't walk into town, did you?" he asked, frowning as he considered just how much activity she might have engaged in.

"I'm afraid I did," Mary admitted. "Is that terrible of me?"

It was hard to chastise her when she looked so healthy and lovely, standing there in her pretty blue muslin dress that matched her blue eyes. Simon relented and made her an offer.

"How about you join me for a bite to eat over at Annie's, and then I'll drive you back to the boarding house so that you don't walk all the way back on your own?"

"Oh, I couldn't impose," Mary protested. "Surely you must be quite busy." Again, she looked at the saloon."

"I have the time," he assured her, offering her his arm. Like the polite woman she was, she took it, and he was able to guide her in the other direction, heading toward the little town restaurant. "Consider it a prescription from your doctor. You need some food in you and then a less taxing way back home. I won't hear of you doing anything else.

Mary smiled up at him. "Well, if you insist."

"I do," he assured her, guiding her into the restaurant. "Annie, a table for two?"

"Sure, Doc," Annie called to him as she cleared plates off a recently abandoned table. It wasn't the normal rush hour, and the place was empty. "Sit anywhere you like."

Simon led Mary to a table near the window that would allow them to look out on the street while they ate. Pulling out her chair, he waited while she seated herself, and then he rounded the table to join her on the other side, taking his hat off and hooking it on the back of his chair.

"Annie is known for her homemade rolls and stew," Simon told Mary. "Or if you've had that quite a bit since coming to town, you could try the roast chicken and potatoes. Everything here is good. Annie is a wonderful cook."

"My ears are burning," Annie said, walking over to the table and placing a pitcher of water and two tin mugs down in front of them. Her rosy red cheeks glowed as she grinned down at them. Her graying hair was pulled back from her face, and her apron was covered in flour. It was her usual look, and she wore it well.

"What can I say?" Simon said. "I can't sing your praises enough, Annie. This woman keeps a bachelor in good food," he told Mary. "She has saved me from malnutrition."

Mary laughed, pouring the water into her tin cup. "Well, Annie, it seems you do good work here. I would be honored to try your chicken and potatoes if I may."

"The stew for me," Simon told Annie. "And a basket of your rolls?"

"Coming right up," Annie promised. She beamed down at Mary and reached out, patting Mary's stomach. "We'll have a little one among us soon enough, won't we? I had heard that we had an expectant mother in town. That's always a joy. Doc here will take excellent care of you."

As Annie hurried off, Simon looked at Mary to see if she was put off by the cook's familiar way with her. But Mary didn't seem perturbed as she sipped her water and looked out the window, and he was glad to see that. Living in a town like Cripple Creek meant being in everyone's business all the time—for better or for worse. That was just the culture they lived in. Sometimes it worked against them, but for the most part it created a tight-knit community that cared for its own. It was what he liked about the town.

"So," Simon said, as they waited for their food. "How have you been settling in?"

"Very well, I think," Mary replied. "Jessamine is wonderful and makes us feel right at home, even though I know we are creating more work for her. At least Nora can be useful." She patted her stomach. "Less so for me right now, but soon enough."

If he was honest with himself, he really wanted to know more about her. He only knew bits and pieces of her story, and he was curious. But he didn't want to seem too presumptuous. It was already rather unusual for him to ask her to lunch, given that they barely knew each other and he was in charge of her care. She was a widowed expectant mother, and he was a single man. In a town like Cripple Creek, that was bound to draw attention.

So instead of asking about her, he focused on neutral topics. "Have you heard much about the town?"

"No," she said. "But I would love to. I was actually thinking of asking Jessamine if the library might have some old newspapers or books that gave the town's history."

"They do," he told her. "I've read them all—at least, I believe I have. And, of course, I grew up here, living the town's history."

"I would love to hear it," Mary said again. "I'm very interested to learn about this new place."

Simon smiled at her enthusiasm. She seemed to have so much of it, even though he could tell her disposition was quieter than her sister's. Even still, there was a sense of adventure in her eyes and a thirst for knowledge that he appreciated. "Well, the town was founded in 1862, not long after the first settlements out here in Colorado. My family moved out here in 1866, when I was just three years old." He could see her doing the math in her head, and he chuckled. "I'm twenty-five years old."

"Of course," Mary agreed. "Go on."

"My dad was a rancher, and he built a house about ten miles outside of town, on a relatively small little patch of land. At the time, there were four main families that had founded the town. Those were the Johnsons, the Browns, the Lawrences, and the Wilsons."

She stopped him. "The Johnsons and the Browns? Like Beth Brown and Nelly Johnson?"

Simon nodded. "That's right. Beth Brown used to be Beth Wilson, and Nelly Johnson used to be Nelly Lawrence. Beth married the Browns' oldest boy, and Nelly married the Johnsons' youngest boy."

"I suppose that isn't surprising, given that they all grew up here together," Mary mused. "So, really, most people in town are related."

"Yes and no," Simon said. "It looks small around here, but there are more people than you'd think. Over the last twenty years, many families have moved in; they've built up these stores that you see along this main strip, and they've bought land and farmed or developed ranches. Annie, here, she came from out east, actually. When Nelly's mother died, Jack Lawrence wrote away for a bride, and Annie answered his advertisement." Simon chuckled, shaking his head. "I don't think that good old Jack thought he would find himself married to a woman who was bound and determined to start her own restaurant. But they're happy, the two of them."

Mary smiled and took a sip of her water. "It's hard not to be happy with a woman who is skilled in the kitchen, I would assume."

"Too true," Simon agreed, enjoying the easy way she talked back and forth with him, commenting as though she was as familiar with the town and the people as he was. She was really listening to him, taking it all in. He realized suddenly that most people didn't do that. Most people let you talk while they thought of their next thing to say—usually about themselves. But that wasn't what Mary was doing. It was refreshing.

"So, Annie is Jack Lawrence's wife, and his daughter, Nelly, is married to the youngest Wilson boy," Mary repeated. "I'm going to have a time of it remembering all of that, but I suppose it'll become second nature to me at some point."

He chuckled, looking out the window at the people passing each other in the streets. "It does," he assured her. "That's the benefit and the downfall of living in a town like this. You know everyone's business and family tree as well as you know your own."

"The founding families," Mary prompted him. "What was their connection? Why did they settle here?"

"Ah, that's a good story," Simon said, sitting back as Annie walked over with two steaming plates.

Annie placed the stew down in front of him and the roast chicken in front of Mary. "Here we are, then. Can I get you anything else?"

Simon shook his head, eagerly reaching for his fork. "This looks wonderful, Annie, as always. I was just telling Mary here about the history of the town and why your husband dragged everyone out here to settle in what was a forsaken place at the time."

"Ah yes," Annie said, nodding. She clucked her tongue, as though she had been there and was remembering it fondly. She looked down at Mary, wiping her hands on her apron. "My Jack, he wanted an adventure, you see. He was tired of factory work. The long hours, barely making a living wage. Answering to miserly overseers who cared only what you could produce and nothing about who you were. So he got three of his friends together, and he convinced them that they should all move west—out to the open land. There was land for the buying, you see. And at a good price, too. Benjamin Wilson was the friend who could bankroll the adventure. He had just inherited a small sum of money, and he bought four parcels of land." Annie smiled and shook her head. "The rest, as they say, is history. They came out here, and they worked until their backs were breaking, and they created Cripple Creek."

As Annie talked, Simon was watching Mary's face. She was enthralled with Annie's story, and her eyes lit up with her enthusiasm, making her beauty even more apparent. It was actually quite wrong how beautiful he found her. After all, she was a recent widow, carrying the child of her late husband. And he was a man who had no business taking a wife.

"What a success," Mary said, when Annie had told her tale. "To think that all of this here is the product of four men on an adventure who started families and livelihoods out here and turned this place into a home."

"That's Jack, all right," Annie said with a fond smile. "He always tells me that when he saw the mountains in the distance, their peaks covered in snow, and he saw the flat plane stretching out before them and the creek, glistening in the sunlight, running right through the land...he knew that he was home."

Mary clasped her hands together. "Oh, I can't wait to see the creek. It can't be far, can it?"

"It's much too far for the moment," Simon said with a laugh, taking a bite of his steaming stew. The richness of the gravy and the beef warmed him from the inside out, just like it always did. "I believe we'll be saving a trip to the creek for when the little one can join you."

"Best to listen to him," Annie agreed, patting Mary's stomach again. "Doc always knows what's best. How's the stew, Doc?"

"It's like heaven," Simon told her. "You outdo yourself every time, Annie, like the angel you are."

Annie let out a loud laugh, shaking her head at him, affection in her eyes. "Oh, go on, then. Eat up. I'll check on you both shortly."

As Annie headed back to the kitchen, Simon smiled at Mary, watching as she took a small bite of her chicken after blowing on it lightly.

"Mmmm," Mary said, her eyes widening. "It's delicious."

"I told you," he reminded her. "This is Annie's calling. There's no doubt."

Mary's eyes darted toward the kitchen, then back to him. When she spoke, her voice was quiet. "Does Annie have children of her own?"

Simon shook his head. "No. She doesn't."

"How sad," Mary murmured, cutting into her roasted potatoes.

Mary's reaction to his answer was only to be expected. After all, the joys of motherhood were God-given. They were precious to any woman, and they must be particularly on Mary's mind, given her condition. But her sympathy for Annie hit Simon hard, making him realize that he was not keeping his failings at the forefront of his mind nearly well enough. Mary clearly considered it a great sorrow to not have children, and she was hardly alone in that assessment—which was why he had committed to never marrying and consigning a woman to the childless life that would be all he could provide her.

That was his normal mindset, so it was surprising to him to see just how easy it was for him to forget that lately. It almost felt like Mary's reaction was a rejection of him, when he had no cause to think that he had any chance with her. He hadn't even consciously considered pursuing her. Yet here he was, feeling as though he had lost something.

"It seems like she would be a wonderful mother," Mary said, unaware of where Simon's mind had gone. "She has such a warm way about her. And if she had a daughter, she could pass down so many family recipes."

"She's close with Nelly and Jack's other children, Rodney and Paul," Simon said, forcing himself to focus on the conversation they were actually having rather than the one taking place in his head. "Annie has been married to Jack for close to fifteen years now, so she's been in their lives for some time. Jack's first wife, Nancy, died not long after giving birth to Paul—the youngest of the siblings. She was taken with a fever, and Jack was left with a new ranch and a growing town to manage, and he needed help."

Mary's brow unfurrowed, and her concern for Annie seemed to diminish. "You don't have to birth children yourself to love them like your own. I didn't realize that she had been in the Lawrence family for so long."

Simon nodded. "Yes, Annie has been a part of Cripple Creek for more than half of my life, come to think of it. She's like a mother to a lot of people, myself included."

"I can see that you two are close," Mary agreed. "That's nice. I like to see the easiness between you two, and the mutual affection. It's clear you both think very highly of each other."

"To have Annie's approval is quite an honor," Simon said. "It's just occurred to me, though, that I might be worrying your sister, keeping you out longer than she expected. If I do that, Jessamine will not be happy with me."

Mary laughed and shook her head. "It's all right. I don't think they'll worry. I'm sure I make them both anxious with my independence, but I've always been that way, you see. I like to do things for myself. On my own. It gives me a sense of purpose." She placed her hand over her stomach, a look of regret passing over her lovely features. "Of course, I didn't quite think I would be raising a child on my own."

"Don't worry," Simon told her gently, resisting the urge to reach out and cover her hand with his. "You have a whole town behind you now. Jessamine. Me.

Annie. I can guarantee we're all praying for you daily."

"I know that's true," Mary murmured gratefully. "May I ask you a question, though?"

"Of course."

"When I first arrived, Nelly Johnson and Beth Brown approached me. That's how I knew their names when you were talking about the founding families a moment ago."

Simon nodded, picking up his napkin and dabbing at the corners of his mouth. "I know. Jessamine told me the story."

"What do you make of it?" Mary asked. "I'm truly not sure what to think. They both appeared so nice and welcoming, but Jessamine said they were simply fishing for gossip and that they intended to impugn my character."

With a sigh, Simon leaned back in his chair, shaking his head. "I have a great deal of respect for Jessamine," he began. "I truly do. She is a hard worker, and she has built that boarding house—figuratively—with her own two hands. She is a powerful ally and a sincere soul and a godly woman."

"But..." Mary prompted, clearly waiting for the other shoe to drop.

"She may also be a touch sensitive when it comes to those two," Simon said honestly. "And I would tell her the same thing. I know that Nelly and Beth gave her some trouble, and I don't deny that the two of them can be gossips. It's an easy trap to fall into in this town because we do all know each other. I'm sure they were certainly fishing for information and that they were being less than honest when they told you they mistook you for Eliza Mason."

"Jessamine says they both know Eliza Mason well."

Simon nodded. "They do, yes. If they indicated otherwise, that was not truthful. But Jessamine seems to think that their intention is to spread rumors that..." he paused, wondering how to put this delicately to her. "That undermine your reputation."

Mary flushed and looked away. "I see."

"I don't believe you need to worry yourself about that right now," Simon said, trying to reassure her. "There's no reason to think that the two were doing anything other than making up some excuse to talk to you and get the latest gossip, considering they're unlikely to get any information from Jessamine."

"Do you think so?"

Again, Simon had to resist the urge to reach over and take her hand. Even at the bedside of his sickly patients, he never felt such a strong urge to make contact and comfort the person. But he kept his hands where they were, not wanting to add any fuel to the fire of any rumor that might be circulating about Mary.

The best thing that Mary could do was marry again. And soon. Not him, though, of course. He would have to keep his mouth shut and his eyes averted as she accepted the attentions of another man who was lucky enough to be able to provide Mary with the kind of life she deserved—one filled with the joys of children.

He suddenly realized that he was only making himself miserable by lingering in the hope that he had inadvertently attached to Mary. Not to mention that every moment they spent together was another reason for Nelly and Beth to start a rumor that the town doctor was seeking a wife after so many years.

"I do," he said as he finished off his stew. "Are you all done? We should get you back to the boarding house before your sister worries."

# CHAPTER 5

Mary Howard

AUGUST 9, 1888

MARY WALKED ARM IN ARM WITH NORA, STROLLING down the sidewalk that led through the center of Cripple Creek. It was an absolutely beautiful morning, with the sun beaming down on them from a bright blue sky. The Colorado summer was lovely, Mary had decided. Warm, but not sweltering. Clear. Bright. Full of possibility. The mountains in the distance were a striking background, hinting at adventure and possibility. And the whitewashed buildings in the town spoke of quaintness and community and opportunity.

It was amusing to Mary now that when she had arrived days earlier what had struck her most was the dust. There was still dust, of course, because of the dry summer heat, but there was so much more to this town than the dust streaks at the bottom of her skirts after she returned from her now daily walks along the Cripple Creek sidewalks. It was going to be the home where her child grew up, and Mary was excited about that possibility.

"I've been thinking," Mary told her sister. "I know that after the baby is born, its care will demand most of my attention for some time. But I also remember how many women I have seen give birth and then return—out of necessity—to their regular duties almost immediately."

"But that isn't necessary for you," Nora reminded her. "Jessamine and I are running the boarding house very well between the two of us, and we both want you to take your time after the birth and focus on your child. You know that."

Mary nodded, catching a glimpse of Beth Brown and Nelly Johnson up ahead of them. "I do know that. But I am also thinking ahead about what I am going to make out of my life, Nora. God gave me this child, and that is my most important purpose, of course. But I cannot be dependent on you forever, can I?"

"Are you thinking of marrying?" Nora asked, sounding intrigued.

"No!" Mary gasped, laughing out loud. "Nora, how could you say that? Who would I marry?"

"Dr. O'Toole seems rather taken with you."

Mary flushed, looking away from her sister. Her eyes moved back to Nelly and Beth, who were standing close together outside of the general store, talking furtively. It made Mary feel slightly nervous, just because she didn't know if she was the topic of conversation.

"No response?" Nora prompted, not following Mary's gaze toward the two other women as she focused on Mary. "Is that an admission that you know Dr. O'Toole is rather taken with you? Because it is quite obvious to the rest of us."

"Hardly," Mary said, pulling her attention from Nelly and Beth. "Simon—Dr. O'Toole—is simply being a friendly, welcoming member of the community and a dedicated medical professional."

"Oh, is that all?" Nora asked with a laugh. "Is that why he had lunch with you two days ago?"

Mary didn't respond, because she was looking at the man Nora was talking about. And he was coming out of the saloon.

Again.

Mary flashed back to two days ago when she had come across Simon O'Toole at eleven thirty in the morning, walking out of the town's saloon. It had thrown her at the time, but his charming demeanor and his invitation to lunch had sufficiently distracted her from wondering why the man was leaving the saloon before midday. And he certainly hadn't seemed intoxicated.

But she had thought about it a time or two since, and she had wondered if her faith in the man was misplaced. Alfred's problem with alcohol still haunted her, and she knew that she never wanted anything to do with anyone with a tendency to drink —ever again. Not a husband, not a friend, and not a doctor.

Simon turned as he walked out of the saloon, heading toward them without yet seeing them. But then he looked up, and his eyes locked with Mary's. He smiled instantly, his eyes lighting up with the smile like he really meant it.

"Mary," he said, walking up to her. "And Nora. How lovely to see you both this fine morning."

"Hello, Dr. O'Toole," Nora said, replying for both of them when Mary didn't immediately speak. "It's nice to see you as well. How are you?"

Simon was looking at Mary, but he turned his gaze back to Nora. "Please," he said warmly. "Call me Simon. I insist. And I'm quite well, thank you."

Nora and Simon made small talk, but Mary didn't pay it any mind. Her own thoughts were reeling. Simon smelled of alcohol, and it sent her tumbling back in time to days when Alfred would come home, smelling of the same. Alfred smelled of it more strongly than Simon did now, but it invoked the memory all the same, and it turned Mary's stomach. She wanted to turn and run, and only her condition and social proprieties kept her from it.

But it was clear that she wasn't being subtle. Both Nora and Simon sensed that she was uncomfortable and on edge, but Simon, at least, had no idea why.

Nora, on the other hand, seemed to catch on.

"You'll have to excuse us, Simon," Nora said, taking her arm from Mary's and placing her hand at Mary's back instead. "I believe my sister is feeling somewhat under the weather. I think I should take her to sit down."

"Of course," Simon said, becoming immediately concerned. He reached his hand out to take Mary's other arm. "Here. There's a bench just down this way."

Mary recoiled from Simon's touch, and the flash of hurt that came over his face was instant, telling her that her repulsion must be all over her own face.

"I'm fine," Mary said tightly, unable to force her voice to sound normal. "Please, excuse me."

She turned, not waiting for Nora, and began to walk in the other direction, heading back toward the boarding house that was miles away. With every step that carried her away from Simon and the scent of alcohol attached to him, she breathed a little easier. By the time that Nora caught up to her, Mary felt less like she was going to panic and fall apart right there in the street with Beth and Nelly waiting to watch it happen.

"Mary," Nora said, grabbing Mary's arm and stopping her. "I know what you're thinking right now, but you have to know how bad that looked to Simon. He has been nothing but kind to us—more than kind. And you just treated him like he was a leper."

"I couldn't help it," Mary said, her hand trembling as she tucked a piece of hair behind her ear. She closed her eyes, hating what had just come over her. "The scent. The smell of alcohol. I keep seeing him walking out of the saloon. In the morning. Long before it is reasonable to take a drink, if taking a drink is ever reasonable."

Nora took Mary's arm, ushering her further down the sidewalk, away from prying eyes. "Let's get off the main street," she said, guiding Mary off the sidewalk and around the back of the fabric store she had shopped in just two days earlier. "Try to steady yourself," Nora urged Mary.

Mary did try to steady herself, and she managed to bring herself back under control. She drew slow breaths and felt herself return to some semblance of normality, and when she did, a sense of shame settled over her. She didn't second-guess her reaction to Simon or doubt that she had good reason for it. But she did regret being openly rude. Even if the man had a drinking problem, it was no excuse for her to openly shun him in public without explanation. She would have to make that right.

But that was all she would make right. Because her reaction to Simon made her realize that she was far more attached to him than she had realized. She had known that she enjoyed his company and found him to be an attractive man, but she had convinced herself that she had that attraction well under control because she knew that she did not intend to marry. But the intensity of her disappointment showed her that she had been subconsciously entertaining the idea of Simon far more than she had realized.

That had to stop, because she had to commit to her resolution that she would never marry again. She simply could not trust herself. She obviously had something inside of her that was attracted to or susceptible to men with drinking problems, and she would never, ever put herself in that situation again. There had been a time in her life when she had found Alfred charming. Not as charming as Simon, perhaps, but there had been a time when she had looked forward to Alfred coming to her parents' house to court her properly. She had been taken in by him and his story of loss, and she had overlooked so much because she had wanted to be married and she hadn't ever really believed that she would get another offer.

She didn't know if Nora was right about Simon being interested in her. If she was being honest with herself, though, she couldn't trust her judgment. She obviously made poor decisions when it came to men, and just days into being in her new home, she was already falling into the same patterns that had trapped her before. A brand-new town, and she had befriended and even started to develop feelings for a man who regularly visited the saloon, first thing in the morning, and reeked of alcohol before noon.

"Let's go back to the boarding house," Mary said to Nora. "I'm steadier. I'm ready to walk."

"Are you sure that's what you want to do?" Nora asked, and there was a hint of rebuke in her voice. "I don't think that Simon deserved what just happened. Do you?"

"I don't know," Mary said, shaking her head. "But I can't talk to him right now." She looked at her sister, pleading with her through her gaze. "Nora, you understand, right? You know what just happened."

"I know that you saw Simon walk out of the saloon," Nora agreed. "And...he smelled faintly of alcohol. And that made you think of Alfred."

Mary nodded. "Yes. He's a drinker, Nora. I've seen him coming out of the saloon in the morning on more than one occasion. He drinks. I can't have anything to do with that."

"I'm not saying that's not reasonable," Nora said, choosing her words carefully. "Or that I don't sympathize. You've been through a lot this past year, Mary. But I think that this might be a little bit of an overreaction this morning."

The sound of rustling skirts came from behind them. "Hello, ladies. Can we help?"

Mary held back her wince as she and Nora turned to see Beth and Nelly appearing around the corner of the fabric store, their faces openly betraying their eagerness for news.

"It's just us," Nelly said, a bright smile on her face. "Is everything all right? We saw you run off from Dr. O'Toole."

"My sister just felt a bit lightheaded," Nora said, keeping her hand carefully on Mary's arm. "She needed to get some air. But we're fine. Thank you for checking."

Beth walked over to Mary, shaking her head. "Really, dear, in your condition, you should be resting. Not walking about the town. Especially since you have no husband to come and pick you up in his buggy. Really, we must get you a ride back to the boarding house."

Mary felt a rush of anger. She wasn't one who was prone to temper, but it was so clear to her that Beth's intentions were not genuine and that she was being snide when she mentioned that Mary had no husband. Everything about Cripple Creek was so lovely—except for these two women who seemed to have nothing better to do than to mess about in her life and try to make her feel bad for things they didn't understand at all.

"That won't be necessary," Mary told the two women, her sweet smile matching theirs. "By the way, Jessamine was telling me what good friends you are with Eliza Mason. It's so strange, then, that you mistook me for her when I first arrived in town. Isn't that strange, Nora?"

Nelly and Beth looked at each other, then they both let out tittering laughs. "Oh well, that was just a little joke. Nothing to take seriously. We just wanted to get to know you, that's all."

Mary was unamused by their laughs and their explanation. She wanted to make a biting comment about Beth's husband, based on what Jessamine had told her, but Mary wasn't that kind of person. She didn't use people's weaknesses against them, even when they were going out of their way to question her character and motives—and out of their way to remind her that she was a woman with child who had no husband.

"Let's go," Mary said to Nora, not responding to Nelly and Beth. She looked at her sister and nodded to her. "I'm ready to go home."

Nora nodded back, linking her arm with Mary's. "Ladies," Nora said, acknowledging the two women as the sisters walked past them.

As they walked back out of town, down the road to the boarding house, Mary stayed quiet at first. She'd intended to have a nice stroll, perhaps do a bit of shopping, and introduce Nora to Annie's wonderful cooking. Instead, her trip had been cut short after her encounter with Simon and then a confrontation of sorts with Nelly and Beth. The beautiful morning suddenly seemed tainted, and Mary knew that the strength of her disappointment was unduly tied to what she had discovered about Simon. She simply hadn't realized how fond she had become of him over the last few days. But that was over now. She would, of course, apologize to him the next time she saw him for her abrupt departure—she didn't intend to be rude. And she would be cordial with him. But that would be the extent of their relationship, because anything more might lure her back into her apparent tendency to develop feelings for men with alcohol dependencies.

"Nora," Mary said, breaking the silence. "Let's ask Jessamine to help us get the midwife here for a visit sooner rather than later."

Nora nodded, likely unsurprised that Mary was thinking in terms of securing new medical assistance. "We'll talk to her about it when we get home. I'm sure we can arrange it."

Mary was grateful for her sister's support. She knew that Nora thought she was overreacting, and Mary was willing to accept that her reaction in town had been disproportionate. But the steps she took from here on out would be reasonable. She had always planned to meet the midwife before the birth, but it had seemed less urgent with Simon on hand to see to her if something went wrong with her health. Now she would no longer be relying on him, because she knew she wouldn't be able to keep the medical relationship separate from the personal one that had begun to develop between them.

Things would be different now. She was just glad that she had learned who Simon O'Toole was before she had grown any fonder of him than she had. It was a loss, but she had already learned the hard way that making excuses for a man who drank only led to heartache. She wouldn't do that again.

# CHAPTER 6

## Simon O'Toole

SIMON STOOD ON THE SIDEWALK, UNSURE WHAT had just happened and why Mary had reacted to him as though he was repugnant. The look on her face had been one of such pure disdain, and she had recoiled from him when he had reached out to her in concern. Based on their last interaction, two days ago, there was nothing that would explain her sudden aversion to him, and if he was being quite honest, it both hurt and angered him that she would so openly and publicly despise him. He had done nothing to deserve such a reaction. He had taken her to lunch, and they had had a nice time together, and then he had driven her back to the boarding house and made sure that she got inside and settled before taking his leave.

Had rumors upset her since then? Had people started talking about them and wondering if there was more between them than there was? He could see that happening, given how small this town was and how much people seemed to be invested in the good doctor settling down with a wife. But even if she had heard whispers, she couldn't be so upset that she would recoil from his touch, could she?

Simon shook his head and shouldered his pack as he turned to walk away. He had other patients to see to, and he couldn't keep standing like a fool in the middle of town as anyone watching whispered about what he might have done to the expecting newcomer to make her so upset with him. As he walked away, he realized yet again just how much he had liked Mary. Her reaction hurt all that much more because he had been gradually growing used to the fact that he had feelings for her that he had never had for someone else. It had never been that hard to stick to his promise to himself that he would never marry, but the moment that Mary had come to town, she had— without even realizing it—started chipping away at his resolve. He had even allowed himself to consider that because Mary had a child on the way, asking her to marry a man who could not give her more children would be less of a burden. Mary would still get to know the joys of motherhood, and he would love her child as his own.

It seemed foolish now to admit that he had ever thought that way when it was quite apparent that he and Mary couldn't be thinking in two more opposite directions.

Simon rubbed his hand over his morning beard, which had grown in when he failed to shave both yesterday morning and this morning. He knew he looked a bit rough around the edges today because he had been quite busy with patients over the last few days. But surely dark circles under his eyes and two days of beard growth wasn't enough to make him repulsive.

"Simon! Simon, do wait up!"

Simon turned toward the voices and found Nelly Johnson and Beth Brown hurrying toward him. He stifled his sigh, not in the mood for polite chitchat, but he put on a smile and lifted a hand to the two women he had grown up with.

"Nelly," he said. "Beth. Nice to see you both."

"We just had to catch you," Nelly said, taking his arm and drawing him to the side, as though separating them from an imaginary crowd of people.

"What's wrong?" Simon asked. "Is someone ill?"

"Not physically," Beth said. "But there is certainly something wrong with that Mary Howard."

Simon frowned, not understanding. "What are you talking about?" he asked. Then Jessamine's words came back to him, and he immediately became defensive. "If you're about to try to undermine her character, I won't hear of it. You know nothing about her husband, and you shouldn't talk about such things."

"Oh, that's the least of our concerns right now," Nelly told him, her voice just above a whisper, as though they were sharing in some secret together. "Though I must tell you—we do find the story quite suspicious."

"It isn't," he said firmly. "Her husband died. That's the whole story."

"Well, then, why didn't his family take her in?" Beth countered smugly. "That's the way of things, isn't it? If you're married to a man and he dies when you're with child, then his family should make you a home with them. Unless you weren't married to him at all."

Simon's temper flared, and he pinned Beth with a steely gaze that he reserved for very select occasions. "Beth Brown, I don't think that you should be going about town spreading gossip about other people's marriages, given the state of your own."

Beth gasped in shock, her hand flying to her chest. "Simon!"

"That feeling that you just got—that's the feeling that Mary has when you go around saying things about her behind her back," Simon told her. "Come on, Beth. I know your parents raised you better than that. What do we talk about in church every week? Love for our neighbors. Doing unto others what we would have done to us." He shook his head at her. "This gossiping habit you two have developed is way out of hand, and your reputations are suffering for it. It's a far worse look for you than the fact that James hasn't shown his face around town in a year."

Beth crossed her arms over her chest, her face red with anger as she glared at him. "Simon O'Toole, I thought you were a gentleman, but you're no better than what Mary Howard said of you."

Simon felt his stomach lurch. "What did Mary say about me?"

"Oh, now you want us to gossip," Nelly said snippily. "How convenient."

He turned his attention to Nelly, zeroing in on her gray eyes that were a bit too wide for her narrow face. "Nelly, what did Mary say about me?"

"That you're a drunk," Nelly said, putting her hands on her hips in a huff. "And that she wants nothing to do with you."

Simon's blood ran cold. "What?"

"That's right," Beth said, nodding. "We saw her rush away from you, and we just went over to help—to see if she was all right and if there was anything we could do."

Simon bit his tongue, holding back the many snide comments he wanted to make about Beth's attempts to portray her motives as pure.

"We were just about to come upon them when we heard Nora and Mary talking," Nelly said, picking up the story. "Mary was saying that she keeps seeing you come out of the saloon. That you reek of alcohol. That you're a drinker, and she wants no part of you."

Simon felt a bit like he couldn't breathe. Never in his life had he had someone make such accusations against him, and they were so unfounded. Simon had taken a drink exactly once in his life, when he was younger, and it had turned his stomach so much that he had never been tempted by it since. He was a sober man in every way, and he took pride in that, and there was no cause for Mary Howard to be saying otherwise. Why would that even occur to her? He couldn't imagine it. Had he ever acted intoxicated around her? He would swear on his life that he had never given her a single reason to think that he lingered at the bottle, and he resented that she would jump to such conclusions on her own and that she would spread them to others.

Perhaps Mary was no better than Beth and Nelly. He couldn't believe that he had been allowing himself to daydream of what a life with Mary would be like—to question his commitment to remaining a bachelor for his whole life.

"That's nonsense," Simon told the two women sharply. "I never touch a drop of alcohol, and if I hear you or anyone else saying anything different, there will be a price to pay." He had to warn them, or these two would be off spreading the rumors that Mary had generated. "I'm a doctor. I can't have people hearing that I drink to excess. They won't trust me to perform my duties."

"There's no need to take it out on us," Beth said with a little sniff. "We're just telling you what Mary said about you. That's all."

"I know you two," Simon said, pointing at both of them. "We all grew up here, and somewhere along the way, the two of you decided that you were going to become the town gossips. Just trust me when I say you don't want to go spreading rumors about me."

Nelly took Beth's arms, her eyes narrowed. "Simon, you have no cause to talk to us the way you have. Now, if you'll excuse us, we'll go find more polite company." The two women turned their noses up at him and walked off together through the town.

He bit back the urge to call after them and tell them to go home to their children and their duties and make themselves useful. Simon wasn't a mean-spirited man, and for the most part, he liked to stay out of other people's business. Before today it had never occurred to him to call out Beth or Nelly for the way they had been for the last few years, even though it was so different from the two girls he had known growing up. And he had always tried to give them the benefit of the doubt, even after the incident with Jessamine.

Now he wasn't feeling so forgiving, and it wasn't just them either.

It was Mary Howard. With her beautiful blue eyes and her infectious laugh and her resilient attitude. She had said she wanted nothing to do with him because he was a drunk.

It was outlandish. It was almost unbelievable.

Actually...was it unbelievable? Could he really take Nelly and Beth's word that Mary had said those things? After all, they were making up other untrue things about Mary and seemed quite interested in making her look bad.

But then he remembered how Mary had recoiled from him. He remembered how two days ago she had kept looking behind him at the saloon. And he knew that this time anyway, Nelly and Beth had not had to make up their story. Mary Howard was telling people that he, Simon O'Toole, was a drunk.

He dragged a hand down his face, wiping the sweat off his brow. It was a steamy day, by Colorado standards, and his shirt was sticking to him, exacerbating the frustration that was brewing up inside of him.

Simon closed his eyes. He wanted to shout, but that would do little good. Instead, he tried to center himself.

*God, I don't know what lesson you're trying to teach me, but I'm going to try to learn it. This is the first time I've cared enough for a woman to think about changing my mind about everything, and it happened in just days. If this is a sign that I was getting it all wrong, I'm listening.*

After his prayer, he did feel more centered, and he scrubbed his hand over his hair, looking around the street. It was all so familiar. The saloon not far from him. Annie's restaurant just down the way. The general store. The people walking up and down the sidewalks, stopping to chat with each other like the old friends and family that they were. Just half a mile up ahead was the church that everyone would be in tomorrow morning for Sunday morning service. After church, people would gather in each other's homes to share food and companionship. He often went over to the Lawrences' house, where Jack and Annie would put on a wonderful Sunday afternoon spread for their regular visitors.

It was all the same as it had been a few days ago, before Mary Howard had come to town on the afternoon train. And it would all still keep being the same.

She didn't change anything. She was just Jessamine's friend who was staying at the boarding house and who he would see as a patient as needed. The spark that he had felt with her would fade from memory and his life would go back to normal.

He liked his life. He was fine with that.

Mary Howard had been just a hiccup that he would quickly move past. As long as she didn't spread her toxic rumors any further than she already had.

Simon walked back into the saloon and went up to the bar. He leaned his hip up against it, looking around at the otherwise empty room. To be honest, he didn't really know how Stanley kept the place running. There was no one in Cripple Creek who frequented his establishment regularly, and Stan was largely dependent upon the seasonal workforce. But Stan was a nice man, and Simon liked him.

"Simon," Stan said, walking into the bar from the back room, rag in hand. "Did you forget somethin'?"

"No," Simon said, looking at Stan's hyperpigmented skin and tired-looking eyes. "I just stepped in to catch my breath for a moment."

"Sure," Stan agreed, leaning against the bar, worn out from walking into the room.

Stan had Addison's Disease. It was a chronic disorder that had no cure, but that could be managed with a long-term treatment program involving tactics to minimize the nausea and weakness and fainting that Stan suffered.

Stan wasn't going to die from his condition, but Stan was also the kind of man who had spent most of his life being a gun-slinging, rough and tough saloon man who absolutely hated that in his forties, he now suddenly found it hard to keep food down, hard to keep his energy up. He had first come to Simon when he had kept fainting without explanation. It made Stan feel weak and vulnerable, and he had pleaded with Simon to treat him at the saloon, away from the curious eyes of the townspeople who would see him if he was going to Simon's practice every few days.

So Simon had always come to the saloon and treated Stan there. It appeared, however, that had backfired against him.

How many times had Mary seen him going in or out of the saloon and assumed the worst about him?

He shook his head. What kind of person jumped to the worst possible conclusion just based on seeing him walk in and out of a saloon a few times? Not the kind of person he needed to be spending time with.

"Can I get you somethin'?" Stan asked, gesturing around. "I know you don't drink, but I can make some coffee. Or get you some water?"

"I'll get it myself," Simon said, gesturing for Stan to sit down. "You look worn out. Have a seat."

"I'm good," Stan insisted, walking over behind the bar and pouring a tin mug of coffee that he slid over to Simon. "What's on your mind, Doc? I can tell that brow is furrowed over somethin'."

Simon took a long draught of the hot, strong black coffee. "Stan, there's a bit of an issue," Simon said. "It seems like there's a rumor going around that I'm a drunk. A newcomer to town has seen me coming in and out of here at odd hours and jumped to conclusions."

"Well, that isn't right," Stan said, pouring himself a cup of coffee as well. "What newcomers? I only know about those two ladies that are living down at the boarding house."

"Yeah," Simon said, raising an eyebrow. "Exactly."

Stan let out a whistle. "Sometimes it's the ones you least suspect. Well, I'd rather people not know about me, but you need to do what you need to do to clear your name. You have my permission to say that you're coming here to treat me."

"I appreciate that, Stan," Simon said sincerely, finishing off his coffee with a couple of last swallows. "I really do. But I'm hoping I don't have to take you up on it. I'm hoping the rumor is dead in the water."

"But if it's not, that could damage your reputation, couldn't it?" Stan asked. "People don't want a drunk doctor, do they?"

"They don't," Simon agreed, shaking his head. "They really don't. But, again, let's hope it doesn't come to that. After all, rumors only have the power people give them, right?"

Stan nodded, setting his mug down on the bar and scrubbing a hand over his face, taking a deep breath. "I can't tell you how much I miss the old days, Doc. The days before, when I could run this place without exhausting myself. When I wasn't worried about passing out any minute."

"I know," Simon said, feeling genuine sympathy for the man who was struggling just to get through each day right now.

Putting his own troubles to the side, Simon got up and walked over to Stan, clapping the man on his shoulder. "I'm praying for you," Simon said. "God's an even better doctor than I am, Stan. Trust in Him."

"I do," Stan said, nodding gratefully. "I know a lot of people assume that I'm God-forsaken, given my place here. But I'm not. I just need to make a livin' like anyone."

"I don't think you're a God-forsaken man," Simon told him, shaking his head. "I know a lot better than that."

Stan gave him a faint smile. "Thanks. You know... there's something I've wanted to ask you for a while now. Since we're havin' a moment here..."

"Sure, ask away," Simon said.

"Why haven't you ever gotten married?" Stan asked, pouring them both more coffee. "People wonder, you know. You're plenty eligible. A doctor. A decent-looking man. Home of his own near town and a practice. I know there aren't a lot of ladies around here, but any one of them would take you in a heartbeat, wouldn't they?"

Simon chuckled, shaking his head. "Well, since we're having a moment, Stan, I'll give you the real answer. For the first time in my life, I was actually considering courting a woman."

Stan let out a whistle. "Yeah? Who?"

"Mary Howard," Simon said, taking a long drink of his coffee. "There was just something about her. The moment that I saw her, I was taken by her. And it was more than that she was beautiful. She had something else."

"It sounds like you're really taken."

"Was," Simon said, shaking his head. "She's the one who has decided that my coming and going from here means I'm a drunk. She told a couple of people today that she wanted nothing to do with me."

"Ouch."

Simon nodded, staring down into the tin mug of dark liquid. "Yeah, it hurt. I won't say it didn't. But I'm taking it as a sign from God. She was the first woman who made me question my resolve, and it's clear that was the wrong thing for me to be doing."

"What resolve?" Stan asked, leaning back against the wall, coffee tin in hand.

"When I was a kid, I fell off a horse," Simon said, setting his own coffee mug down. "It was out on the ranch. I was riding with my dad. I won't go into details, but it was a bad accident, and well...I'm not able to have children."

It was a harder thing to say than Simon expected. He had never really talked about it with anyone. At the time of the injury, it had been clear that there was damage, but it was his medical training and research over the years he studied to become a doctor that led him to the unshakeable conclusion that he would never be able to reproduce. He was a reasonable enough man to know that didn't truly undermine his masculinity or make him less than. Everyone had medical conditions that they dealt with, and this was his. But he didn't know how Stan would react. Stan was worried about having Addison's disease and how that undermined his own strength and masculinity. Would he look down on Simon the same way he looked down on himself?"

"I'm real sorry about that," Stan said, shaking his head. "That's gotta be a hard thing to deal with."

Simon was pleasantly surprised. Stan didn't seem to judge him at all, and his sympathy was genuine. It was a relief, in a way, to have finally told someone and to have that person react as though it was a normal thing for him to reveal—not some secret that made him a failure or a disappointment.

"I've come to terms with it," Simon said. "But if there's one thing I've always been sure of, it's that I would never take a wife and deprive her of the joy of motherhood. I never thought it was fair to ask that of a woman, whether we married for love or for a partnership or any reason. A woman should have the chance to bear children, and I can't give that to her."

"But Mary Howard changed your mind?"

"She almost had me going back on my commitment to that," Simon admitted. "I rationalized it because she's already with child. Her husband passed, you know, some months ago. And I thought...she already will know the joy of motherhood, and I felt this connection to her." Simon finished the last of his coffee and pushed away from the bar. "It was a foolish thought. One that I'm glad God took out of my mind before I could follow through on it."

"Well, you don't want a wife who starts jumping to conclusions and hurting your reputation," Stan agreed, shaking his head back and forth. He looked pensive. "But, if you want my two cents, don't write any of it off, Doc. Not her. Not marriage. You just never know what life has planned for you, and everyone can make their own choices. Life is too short to be writing off opportunities before they even show up."

Simon thought about that for a moment, recognizing that there was a lot of wisdom in what Stan said. After all, look at Jack and Annie Lawrence. They had found each other later in life, and Annie had never had kids of her own, but Simon knew that she loved Jack, and the two were happy together.

"Maybe you're right," Simon told Stand. "Maybe I shouldn't write off marriage forever in all circumstances. But I'm right about Mary."

Stan nodded. "Yeah. You just might be right there. I can't deny that."

"Yeah," Simon said, pushing his mug over toward Stan. "Thanks for the talk, Stan. It really helped clear my head."

"Hey, anytime, Doc," Stan said with a smile. "You know you're always welcome here." His smile grew grim. "I'll save a couple dozen drinks for you next time, so you can live up to your reputation."

Simon chuckled, shaking his head. "I'm glad you have that sense of humor, Stan. It suits you."

"Some days, a sense of humor is all a man has."

Simon clapped Stan on the shoulder and took his leave of the saloon, heading for his next patient. He walked with his head held high, taking comfort in the fact that people like Stan knew who he really was and wouldn't be swayed by anything Mary Howard said. That gave him the confidence to put Mary Howard out of his mind. She was in the past—a momentary lapse in judgment that one day he would laugh about. That was it.

# CHAPTER 7

## Mary Howard

AUGUST 10, 1888

MARY HAD ALWAYS LOVED SINGING IN CHURCH. Something about the way that the voices all blended together into a disorganized but beautiful harmony just warmed her soul. She sang with all her heart, praising God with her new community—and with Nora and Jessamine on either side of her, their own voices joining in.

The sermon on Sunday morning spoke to her too. It was a message of hope and commitment. A reminder that God had a plan for every part of their lives and that even when hard times came, God was there, sheltering them. Mary listened with her hands on her stomach, soothing the sleeping child within who would soon be born into a world where he would be entirely dependent upon Mary. She didn't know what his world would look like, other than that she would be devoted to making it the best world possible for her child. And she was trusting in God to help her do that.

As the pastor spoke, Mary found herself glancing over at Simon. He was sitting on the other side of the small building, seated by himself but in the same row as a family with three kids. Every once in a while the youngest—a boy who looked like he was about three years old—would look over at Simon and imitate the way he was sitting. It was cute how the little boy looked up to the doctor, and Mary caught Simon smiling at the boy several times, encouraging him. Not once did Simon look over at her, making it quite clear that her reaction to him the morning before had sufficiently put him off.

It made her sad, she realized.

And conflicted.

There was so much good in Simon. She had seen it herself in the way he patiently and diligently cared for her when she had first arrived. His relationship with Annie in the restaurant. Jessamine had only good things to say about him as well. Mary believed that he was a kind man who cared about his patients and had a good sense of humor and a heart that was in the right place. He sang in church with real feeling, and he bowed his head reverently in prayer with the rest of the congregation.

And so had Alfred. Jessamine had promised Mary that she was mistaken about Simon—that he wasn't a drunk. He wasn't even a regular drinker. Jessamine had told Mary that she was overreacting and that she needed to give Simon the benefit of the doubt.

That's what people had told her about Alfred, too, when she'd first had her suspicions. So many people wanted to believe the best about Alfred—including her—and together they had all ignored the red flags that they should have seen earlier on. They had found ways to explain them and rationalize, and Mary had ended up married to a man who put his need for drink above their finances, above her, and ultimately above his own life.

She wasn't going to let that rationalization happen again, no matter how much she wished that she could go back in time before she had realized who Simon was. It would be so nice to know that she was going to talk to him after the service and that he would check on her and perhaps they would make plans that he would come by the boarding house later in the week.

Mary sighed, reining in her thoughts for the thousandth time since she had met Simon. She was imagining him courting her. That was the only description of the scenarios she was playing out in her mind. She wanted Simon to court her—or at least she had before she had found out about his drinking. What was wrong with her that she could so quickly forget her resolve to be independent?

The church service ended, and Mary said a small prayer asking God for forgiveness after letting her mind wander to earthly things during the last ten minutes of the service. She rose with Jessamine and Nora, filing out of the church with the rest of the congregation. Annie Lawrence waved to her from across the building, and Mary smiled and waved back. The moment that Mary stepped outside, Beth Brown was at her side.

"Oh," Mary said, startled. "Hello, Beth. How...nice to see you."

"Mary," Beth said with a tight smile. "It's come to my attention that perhaps I haven't acted with as much... grace as I should, welcoming you to our town."

Now Mary was truly surprised. "Oh?"

"Yes," Beth said, her smile growing even tighter. "We all have our little things about our lives that we don't like others to talk about, right?"

"I suppose we do," Mary agreed, sure that Beth was referencing her own husband but unsure what Beth might think that Mary wouldn't want to talk about. Beth didn't know about how Alfred had passed. No one did except Jessamine and Nora, and they wouldn't have told anyone.

"I should think that's a lesson you've learned too," Beth continued, looking over at Simon. "What Nelly and I overheard you say about Dr. O'Toole...well, it's really not appropriate, is it?"

Mary felt a pull of dread at her heart. "What exactly did you overhear me say?"

"Well, just that he's a drunk, and you want nothing to do with him," Beth said, her eyes wide and innocent. "Remember?"

Mary did remember, and she felt sick when she realized that Beth and Nelly must have been listening to her conversation with Nora before they drew the two sisters' attention. "Beth, what you heard was not—"

"True?" Beth interrupted. "No, I don't think it is."

"It wasn't meant to be heard," Mary said, not commenting on whether it was true. "I don't have any intention of causing a problem for Sim—for Dr. O'Toole."

"Well, I don't think that's how he sees it," Beth said, scrunching her nose up. A young girl ran up to Beth, grabbing her hand and tugging. "Just a minute, Sarah," Beth chided. "Manners, dear. Excuse me, Mary. I need to see to my family."

"Wait," Mary said, her voice sharp. "Beth, did you tell Simon what you heard me say?"

"Of course," Beth said solemnly. "I think we all need to do better about not assuming the worst of each other and not spreading rumors. That's what I got from today's sermon, and now I've made my part right with you. You'll have to make things right with Simon on your own."

Feeling momentarily lightheaded, Mary closed her eyes as Beth walked off with her daughter. A rush of shame came over her as she imagined how Simon must have felt when he heard Beth's version of what Mary had said. No matter how true her words were, it would have been hurtful to hear them, and she had genuinely never intended to hurt him.

"Nora," Mary said, walking over to where her sister was talking with several townspeople, looking lovely in her lavender Sunday best. "A word?"

Nora walked a few feet away with her, brow furrowed with concern. "What's wrong?"

"Nelly and Beth heard our conversation yesterday and relayed it to Simon," Mary said, her voice lowered. "Beth told him that I called him a drunk and said I wanted nothing to do with him."

Nora's face fell, her shoulders slumping in disappointment. "Oh, Mary."

"I would never have wanted him to hear that," Mary said, covering her face with her hands. "Why can't those two keep their mouths shut?"

"You should ask yourself the same question," Nora said gently. "Words have power, Mary. You know you should never have called Simon a drunk, no matter what you worried might be true. Jessamine has said his character is unreproachable."

Mary felt like she'd had this conversation with Nora a hundred times over the last twenty-four hours. She understood where her sister was coming from, and Mary had learned to trust Nora's judgment in many things. But she just couldn't shake the memory of everyone wanting to see the best in Alfred and making excuse after excuse for him.

"Maybe you should talk to Simon," Nora suggested, nodding toward the doctor, who stood talking with Jack and Annie and several others. "You could just ask him about the saloon. See what he says. Tell him that you're sorry you ever questioned his character where others could hear you."

Mary was torn. Part of her longed to go do just that and hope that they could clear it up. The other part of her told her to stay as far away as possible and protect her heart.

"I couldn't help but overhear," Jessamine said, walking up to the sisters. "Mostly because I was actively listening." She gave Mary a stern look. "I love you like you're my own sister by birth, Mary Howard, but you've hurt my friend. If you don't make it right, you're no better than Beth and Nelly, spreading rumors that hurt people's reputations without any basis for the rumors."

"I have basis," Mary started to argue, before stopping herself. She nodded, knowing that she had no real argument to stand on. She shouldn't have said what she said, and the fact that she still believed that Simon was a drinker didn't change the fact that she shouldn't have said what she said. "I'll talk to him."

Jessamine smiled and touched her arm. "Good luck."

Taking a deep breath, Mary walked across the churchyard. Simon glanced at her as she approached, and the easy smile on his face disappeared. He looked instantly wary and not at all happy to see her.

Mary stepped up to him anyway. "Could we walk for a moment?"

"I actually have a great deal to do at the practice this afternoon," Simon said, causing the others to avert their eyes from the awkward encounter. "I'm sorry. Perhaps another time."

"It's important," Mary said, pleading with him with her eyes. "It'll only take a moment."

"Are you feeling well?" Simon asked, his eyes flickering down to her swollen stomach.

"Quite."

"Then I'm afraid I need to see to my practice."

Mary was about to give up and walk away, but then Annie touched Simon's arm and gave him a look. He gave her one right back, but then some communication seemed to flow between the two, and Simon sighed, surrendering to Annie's silent instructions.

"I suppose I have a moment," Simon told Mary.

He stepped away with her, but notably he did not offer her his arm. He was looking quite handsome, dressed in a blue shirt and dark brown pants. He was wearing his customary cowboy hat as well, keeping the August sun off his face as they walked to a more private space.

"I spoke to Beth," Mary said quietly. "And I want to say that I owe you an apology for what she overheard me say. It was said in the heat of the moment and not intended to be overheard by anyone."

"Do you apologize for being overheard or for what you said?" Simon asked, stopping them as they walked and turning to face her.

"It was much too harsh," Mary admitted. "I should never have said it where anyone could hear me."

Simon smiled, but there was no humor in it. "There it is again," he said. "You're apologizing for making a statement at an inopportune time where you could be overheard. I haven't heard you say that you know you were mistaken about what you called me."

It was clear to Mary that Simon was not just upset— he was angry with her. His eyes lacked the warmth that had always been there before, and she didn't quite know how to take him when he was so distant and formal with her.

"Simon," Mary said, searching for the words to say.

"Dr. O'Toole," he corrected her. "You're my patient, Miss Howard. That is the extent of our relationship."

His words felt like a slap in the face, even though she had thought she had come to the same conclusion that their relationship would be strictly professional. To see and hear him say it with such definitive confidence, though, was something else altogether. He wasn't listening to her. He wasn't interested in hearing what she had to say about what had happened.

This anger. Alfred had displayed anger when confronted with his wrongdoings too. When she would challenge him on how much he drank, he would get defensive with her—just like Simon was getting defensive with her now.

That realization made the conversation a little easier for Mary because it removed some of the conflict she felt.

"Dr. O'Toole," Mary said, using his formal title. "I know what I saw. I know what I smelled on you. You don't know everything there is to know about my past, and I don't feel obligated to share that with you. But just know that I recognize the signs when I see them. And while I should not have been so blunt or so careless in my statement, I don't apologize for my assessment."

"Oh really?" Simon said, crossing his arms over his chest. "So you stand by your conclusion that I am a drunk?"

"That you drink," Mary said, nodding. "Yes, I do. That you drink frequently. Enough to be called a drinker."

"And what led you to that conclusion?"

Mary gestured toward the town. "I saw you. You come and go from the saloon frequently. Even in the morning. And you smell like...drink."

"Right now?"

"No, not right now. But yesterday you did."

Simon gave her a long, appraising look. "What if I told you that I had an explanation for that? That if I told you that explanation, you would see that you're wrong about what you've assumed about me?"

"I don't know," Mary said honestly. "I think it would be difficult for me to believe that."

"Why?"

"Because of how defensive you're being," Mary told him. "Why are you so defensive if there has been an innocent misunderstanding?"

"I'll tell you why," Simon said. "Because I was fond of you, Mary."

His words hit her hard. His use of her first name again—signaling the easy intimacy they had developed. The passion with which he spat out the sentence. The hurt look on his face.

"I foolishly thought that you and I had a mutual affection and respect for each other," he continued. "Clearly I was mistaken about that because it took you no time and no evidence to jump to the worst conclusion possible and state that you wanted nothing to do with me."

She had hurt him, Mary realized. She knew that she had, of course, because it was always hurtful to hear someone say something negative about you. But it went deeper than that. She had hurt him in a way that it wouldn't have hurt him if someone else had made the accusation.

Because he cared for her.

Nora had been right. Dr. Simon O'Toole had been quite taken with her.

She didn't expect the rise of emotion that produced within her, and she took a step back, the conversation suddenly overwhelming.

"I'm not going to give you the explanation that would clear this up," Simon said. "Because to do that, I would have to betray the confidence of a person who thinks the best of me rather than the worst of me. And I choose not to do that." He shook his head, looking away from her for a moment. "To think how close I came to giving you more of me than I've ever given someone. Only to find this out—just in time."

"Simon…"

"Dr. O'Toole," he said, correcting her again. "Miss Howard, I wish you the very best health. Please let me know if you need my medical services at any time.

But I trust the midwife will be able to assist you from here."

Mary felt tears prick at her eyes. "Simon, please...."

But she didn't know how to finish the sentence. Did she trust him? Was his promise that there was an explanation enough? Had it been enough with Alfred? Her heart and her head were in conflict, and she didn't know what to say to him. She didn't know how to decide what she wanted to do.

"God bless, Miss Howard," Simon said, giving her one more long glance before he walked back to the churchyard, leaving her standing alone.

AUGUST 13, 1888

Mary sat in the boarding house's west sitting room, reading. It was late afternoon, and the summer sun was streaming in through the windows. Around her, she could hear the noises of the boarding house. Dishes clanking in the kitchen, preparing for dinner. Feet moving up and down the hallways and stairs. Voices echoing through the walls.

She sighed, shifting in her chair. All day, Mary had been uncomfortable, unable to get settled into any sitting position that took the weight off her lower back without putting her legs to sleep. There was a burning sensation in her chest that wouldn't go away, and her exhaustion had suddenly overtaken her in a way she hadn't experienced since the early months of her pregnancy.

A nap sounded delightful, but the midwife was supposed to come by for a visit shortly. They hadn't yet met, and Mary could tell that it would be time for the baby to be born any day now. It was important that Mary meet the midwife and make sure that they were all on the same page. After all, she couldn't count on Simon as a backup now.

As usual, the thought of Simon plummeted her mood even further. Over the last days, she had thought about Simon so often that she was exhausted from the mental loop in her head. There was no getting off the loop. Every time she decided that she had judged him harshly, she thought of Alfred and the excuses that she had made for him, and then every time she thought of Alfred, she remembered that Simon wasn't Alfred and everyone believed he was a good man with strong morals and an unrelenting work ethic.

The last stop on the loop was always the realization that it didn't matter what she decided about Simon. He had very clearly decided that he was done with her, and he was not shy about it. That Sunday in the churchyard, he had told her just how much she had hurt him, and since then, he hadn't attempted to make any contact with Jessamine or with Mary. And Mary hadn't gone into town once, both afraid to bump into Simon and too tired to do as much walking as she had done previously.

All week, she had been sitting in the boarding house, thinking, worrying, and keeping herself as calm as possible with prayer and Jessamine and Nora's comforting company.

A sharp pain shot across her abdomen, and Mary gasped with shock. She'd had twinges and discomforts before, but nothing that was so sudden and powerful. Her hand left the book of poems she was holding and gripped the arm of the chair as her eyes squeezed shut. It was hard to breathe, and she felt almost dizzy. Then the pain hit her again, just as sharply, and it lasted even longer. Then a third pain.

She had read about birthing. She had talked to women who had given birth. To some degree, Mary knew what to expect, and she didn't think it was supposed to be like this. So fast. So sudden. So abrupt.

"Nora!" Mary shouted, holding onto the chair as her muscles tensed and seized. "Nora, something is happening!"

"Mary?" Nora called back, coming rushing toward the sitting room. "What is it?" Nora stopped short in the doorway, staring at Mary in shock. "Oh, Mary! Is he coming now?"

Mary nodded, gripping her stomach, her breaths coming in short, abrupt gasps. "Yes. Now."

"The midwife isn't here!" Nora lamented, rushing over to Mary and taking her hand. "Hold onto me. Hold on. We have to try to wait for the midwife."

Mary shook her head. "There's no waiting, Nora. You need to get hot water and towels now."

"We need Simon."

"No," Mary said sharply, and not just because the pain was hitting her again, worse than ever. "Simon isn't to know. We're doing this on our own, Nora. You and me and Jessamine. God is going to have to guide us."

*God,* Mary prayed silently. *Please, please, please. Guide us. Bring my baby into this world safely.*

# CHAPTER 8

## Simon O'Toole

SIMON CAREFULLY PLACED THE LAST STITCH IN little Harry Brown's arm, noting with admiration how the seven-year-old boy gritted his teeth and bore the pain. Harry had been climbing trees with his little sister, and when she got scared about getting down, Harry had tried to help her—only to fall down himself and split open his elbow.

Beth Brown had called for Simon, and he'd hurried out to tend to the boy, who was keeping a very stiff upper lip during the whole process.

"There we are," Simon said, bandaging up the elbow to keep the stitches dry and offering Harry a reassuring smile. "All set now. You'll be as good as new before you know it."

"Thanks, Dr. O'Toole," Harry said, standing up. "That wasn't so bad."

Simon smiled and ruffled the boy's hair before sending him off to show off his wounds to his sister. Then Simon turned toward Beth, packing up his bag as he watched her watching her oldest examine his bandages.

"Beth?"

She turned her head to meet his gaze, her own defensive already before he said anything. "Yes, Simon?"

"How are you doing out here?"

"Perfectly fine."

Simon sighed and shouldered his bag, walking over to Beth and looking her dead in the eye. "Beth. I know you would have preferred not to have me come out here. But maybe it's a good thing that I did. You can't keep running this place on your own."

"I'm not on my own."

He raised an eyebrow at her, waiting.

"Simon, I don't want to discuss this with you," Beth told him, stooping to pick up her youngest and settling the little girl on her hip. She handed her daughter one of the rolls she had been baking. "What we do here is our business, and while I'm sure you mean well, it's not helpful."

"Do you ever hear from James?"

Beth's eyes flashed with anger. "Simon, do not press this issue."

"So it's all right for you to get involved in everyone else's business, but no one should get involved in yours?" Simon asked, tilting his head and pursing his lips. "That doesn't make too much sense to me. Does it to you?"

"I don't get involved in other people's business."

"Beth, it's your only hobby," Simon said. "And I think it became your only hobby when you and James started having problems, and you took Nelly along with you for the ride. Because I don't remember you being quite so insufferable when we were younger." He smiled a bit to ease the sharpness of his words. "I'm a friend. I can help. James has obviously gotten spooked and left town. We need to get you help out here."

"Simon," Beth said, and he couldn't imagine that whatever followed his name would be good when she said his name that way.

He didn't get to find out, though. There was a sharp knock at Beth's door, and then Jessamine's voice, calling his name.

"Simon! Simon!"

Startled, Simon rushed to the door and pulled it open, taking in the sight of a harried and disarrayed Jessamine. "What's wrong?" he demanded. "What is it? Is it Mary?"

Jessamine nodded. "Yes. You have to come right now. She gave birth. On her own. The baby is fine, but Mary—there's something wrong."

Simon felt his heart leap into his throat, and he had to intentionally calm himself and take on his doctor persona. He didn't know what had come over him when he saw Jessamine, but he had just known that Mary was in trouble, and the panic that had come over him was the same kind of panic he felt when his mother had fallen ill.

Nothing else mattered. He had to get to her.

"Let's go," Simon said, gripping his bag tighter and looking back at Beth. "Beth, this conversation isn't over, but I've got to go."

She nodded, but he barely noticed as he hurried out the door with Jessamine and followed her to her buggy. They both climbed up front in the driver's seat, and Jessamine snapped the reins, sending the horse running down the street.

"Tell me everything," he said as they flew as fast as the buggy would go over the bumpy roads. "What happened?"

"Mary went into labor out of nowhere," Jessamine said, artfully handling the reins at the same time that she told the story. "She'd been uncomfortable and restless all day. I knew she was getting close, but not that close. There was no time for the midwife to get there. Labor was under an hour, and it was brutally painful."

Simon closed his eyes for a moment, shutting out the thought of Mary screaming in agony. "Blood?"

"So much," Jessamine said. "We took care of her, Nora and I. We managed to get the baby birthed, and she cried—"

"She?"

"She."

Simon wondered if Mary was surprised. She had been so sure it would be a boy. But that wasn't the kind of thing that mattered right now. "The baby is fine?"

"We think so," Jessamine said. "Nora and I. We're not doctors. But the baby was fine when I left. Except—"

"Except what?"

"She can't nurse. Mary is barely conscious. She's feverish. She's thrashing around unless Nora lies beside her, and when she thrashes, there's more blood. She's pale."

"Where is the midwife?" Simon demanded. "Why did she never come?"

"She was supposed to visit this afternoon, but there was no set time. She had others to tend to as well," Jessamine explained, her voice lurching as the buggy hit a hole in the road and rattled dangerously.

"We need to get there safely," Simon reminded her. "Slow down. We're no good to Mary if we're in a ditch."

"Simon, I'm afraid," Jessamine said, looking over at him with eyes that betrayed just how sincere her words were. "I'm afraid that she's not going to be alive when we get back to the boarding house."

"Why didn't you send for me sooner?" Simon asked, his own fears clawing at him.

Jessamine shook her head. "It all happened so fast. Nora wanted to call you at the beginning, but Mary said no."

"She said no?"

"She felt guilty," Jessamine said. "For how things ended with you two. She cared about you, Simon. She really, really cared about you, and she was just too scared."

"Stop talking about her in the past tense," Simon said. "She's going to be fine, Jessamine."

Jessamine nodded, snapping the reins to make the horses go faster again. They were both barely hanging onto the seat of the buggy as it rattled through town. "Simon, Mary's husband died because he had an alcohol dependency."

"What?"

"He drank himself into all sorts of trouble. Ruined their finances. Lied to her. And he drank on the job, which caused the accident that killed him."

Simon looked over at Jessamine, nearly losing his balance as she whipped the buggy around a sharp turn in the road. "That's why...?"

Jessamine nodded. "She liked you. More than she would even admit to herself. She would find reasons to bring up your name around the house, just in common conversation. When you dropped her off that one morning, she was glowing. She had feelings for you, Simon, and then she got scared."

It all made so much more sense with that context. No, he still didn't like that Mary had judged him so harshly, but he understood now that it had very little to do with him and everything to do with past traumatic situations that she likely hadn't fully dealt with yet. Her husband had been a drunkard, and his illness had taken him from Mary. Of course she would be sensitive to any indication that another man that she might have feelings for was the same. Of course she would have trouble trusting Simon when he reassured her, because her husband must have assured her time and time again—only to fail her.

Mary had feelings for him.

The words rattled around in his head, and he wasn't sure where to settle them. Whether to grab and hold onto them or whether to shove them out of the way where he wouldn't have to deal with what they meant and how he felt about them.

Since Sunday, Simon had worked hard to keep Mary Howard out of his thoughts altogether. To consign her to the brief hiccup she had been in his life and to return to the contentment that he felt in going about his work and being part of the Cripple Creek community.

It hadn't really worked, but he had been getting better and better at it with each day that had passed. She still cropped up in his thoughts every hour, but he wasn't ruminating about the explosive end to their relationship that had never really started. He still thought about the way her blue eyes twinkled when she was amused and the way wisps of her chestnut hair were always escaping out of her careful up-do. Her easy laugh. The way she listened when other people were talking, like she really cared about what they were saying. Her ability to take her situation in stride and her determination to be independent and capable all on her own.

Actually, he hadn't done a good job of putting her out of his mind at all, he realized. She had been with him every day, and while he had kept up his mental insistence that things were done between them, he wondered if he had ever truly believed it.

When Jessamine had shown up at Beth's house and told him about Mary, he hadn't even stopped to question it. He was going to her. And it wasn't just because she was a patient in need. She was Mary, and there was just no staying away.

"I love her," Simon told Jessamine just as they were pulling up to the boarding house. "I can't help it. I love her, Jessamine."

"Don't tell me," Jessamine said, pointing toward the boarding house. "Go in there and save her life so you can tell her yourself."

Simon gripped his bag, jumping down from the buggy. As he ran inside, Jessamine stayed back to see to the horses, which she had just ridden harder than she should have. Nora met Simon at the door, ushering him inside, her face pale and her eyes wide with fear. There was a baby, swaddled in her arms, a head full of dark hair peeking out the top.

"Simon. Thank God you're here."

"Where is she?" he asked, even as he looked at the babe in her arms. His heart swelled at the sight of the little crop of hair, and he reached out, gently touching the dark strands. "Is the baby...?"

"The baby is strong and healthy," Nora assured him. "Mary is up the stairs. I'll take you to her. Simon, she's not well."

"I'll help her," he promised. *Please, God, help me to do that.*

Simon followed Nora up the stairs, and Nora let him into a bedroom where he found Mary lying in the bed, so pale that cold fingers of dread wrapped around his heart. Her breathing was labored, and her eyes were closed.

He walked over, throwing propriety out the window as he sat down on the edge of the quilt and took her hand in his, bringing it to his lips.

"Mary," he said softly. But her eyes stayed closed and she didn't stir. Simon closed his eyes, praying over her aloud. "God, please put your hand over Mary. Protect her. Allow me to heal her. I need her. Her little girl needs her, Father. She is not done here."

"Simon."

His name was just a whisper—the faintest of sounds on her lips.

But he opened his eyes, and he found her trying to open hers and look at him. He kissed her fingers again and lifted a hand to her cheek, feeling how flushed her skin was.

"I'm here, Mary," he said, stroking her soft, over-heated skin. "It's all right now."

"Simon, my daughter..."

"Shhhh," he said, standing up. "Don't worry yourself. You'll see her shortly. She is doing so well, Mary. She's strong and she's healthy, and she has so much dark hair. You'll never believe it."

Out of the corner of his eye, he saw Nora in the hallway, staying out of the line of sight so that Mary wouldn't see the baby and ask for her. Tears were running down Nora's cheeks, silent and desperate. She loved Mary, too, and she was holding a little girl who needed Mary more than anyone.

Losing her wasn't an option.

It didn't take much to see that Mary was suffering a hemorrhage—an all too common side effect of birth that could be terribly deadly. He had never dealt with a situation like this before. In fact, he had never been called to a birth before, as women generally preferred female midwives to male doctors in their most vulnerable moments. But he was good at what he did, and he had an instinctive way of working with the body, often just knowing what to do to get it to respond.

She groaned a bit, turning her head back and forth. She didn't appear to be fully aware of what was happening or, sometimes, even who he was, but Simon talked to her as he treated her, telling her what he was doing and constantly promising her that she was going to be all right.

As he was finishing, Jessamine appeared in the doorway, flushed and frantic but ready to help. "What do you need?" Jessamine asked. "What can I do?"

"Boiled water, towels, and alcohol," he rattled off to her. "Now."

"Alcohol?'

"It's a sterilizer," he said, looking back at her. "Are you questioning me, Jessamine? I'm not having a drink."

"I didn't mean it that way," Jessamine said, speaking just as sharply to him. "I need to know what kind you want, Simon."

"The strongest you have."

She disappeared, and Simon worked feverishly to warm Mary's feet, which were ice cold, to try to draw the fever out of her. He gave her some pain medication to make her more comfortable and to keep her somewhat sedated so that she didn't thrash or startle or stress herself into a worse situation than she was already in.

When Jessamine returned, Simon had Jessamine replace the blood-soaked cloths with fresh ones so that they could determine the severity of the hemorrhage. There was still bleeding, but Jessamine said she thought it might have slowed. But Simon knew it was still far too much.

"I need to examine her further," Simon told Jessamine. "I need to see if there is something that is preventing the body from healing itself the way that it should. Or if something has been torn."

"She wouldn't want that," Jessamine said. "Isn't there something you can give her to stop the bleeding?"

"I've given her what I can," Simon said, dragging a hand over his face. "But we can't just rely on that. I know that she wouldn't want me to be the one to examine her, Jessamine, but her life is on the line."

"Jessamine!" Nora called from the hallway. "The midwife is here! She's arrived!"

"Send her up immediately," Jessamine called back, pressing a hand to her chest. "Let the midwife examine her," Jessamine told Simon. "Together, you'll help her. I know you will. Look at her. She already looks more stable. Doesn't she? Don't you think she looks more stable?"

Simon looked over at Mary's face, and it was with some amount of relief that he acknowledged that she did look less flushed and distressed. Of course, he had given her pain medication which would ease her discomfort and let her rest easier, but he chose to believe that her appearance was also an indication that she was stabilizing. That at least she wasn't still falling further and further out of their reach.

He walked to her and sat beside her again, taking her hand in his. He pressed her palm to his cheek, leaning into her touch. "Mary," he said softly. "Stay with us, Mary. Fight. You're so strong. I've seen how strong you are, and you're going to get through this."

The midwife walked into the room, and Simon stood up, striding over to her.

"Simon O'Toole. I'm a physician. Her bleeding, we believe, has slowed somewhat, but it hasn't stopped. I haven't examined her. We were waiting for you to do that."

The midwife, a pinched-looking woman in her late forties, nodded her head. "Martha Michelson. You've stabilized her. That's good. Let me see to her."

Simon stood up by the top of the bed, holding Mary's hand as Martha examined her. He kept his eye on her breathing, and as he was holding her hand, he kept his fingers at the pulse in her wrist to monitor her heartbeat. It was far weaker than he would have hoped.

Martha looked up at him, her face grim. "She's in trouble. This is going to be a long night."

"Losing her isn't an option," Simon told the woman, the emotion thick in his voice. "Whatever we have to do—we'll do it."

# CHAPTER 9

Mary Howard

August 14, 1888

Mary's body felt heavy. Her eyes didn't want to open. Her hands didn't want to move. Her leg was in an uncomfortable position, but she couldn't seem to make it stretch out to ease the strain on her muscles. Her tongue was thick and her lips dry. She struggled to find context for where she was. What day it was. Why she was lying here. What had happened to her. Her memories were fuzzy and disorienting, and her body hurt. It didn't just hurt— every part of her ached.

As she lay there, eyes closed, searching her mind for

something that would make sense to her, memories started to come back like elusive wisps. Sitting in the western sitting room, reading. Her discomfort that had quickly turned into unimaginable pain. The flurry of activity as Jessamine and Nora ushered her up to the bedroom and told her that the time had come to bring her baby into the world.

Prayer. So much prayer as she had pushed and fought against the invisible forces that were seemingly pressing back against her to keep her from bringing her daughter into the world. The pain. The disorientation.

And then that cry.

Her baby. Her baby had been born. She knew somehow that it was a girl, even though she had spent nine months convinced that she was having a baby boy.

Where was her daughter? What had happened to her?

She could remember Nora taking her, washing her, bundling her. Where had Nora gone with her? Why wasn't her daughter here beside her as she lay in bed?

Mary tried to force her eyes open, but it was as though heavy weights were attached to her eyelids, keeping the world around her dark. She tried to speak, but her lips were sluggish, and she couldn't tell if she was forming words or just groaning.

More memories were coming back. So much more pain and blood—blood everywhere. Too much blood. And she felt so weak and helpless through it all. She had fought as hard as she could, straining to stay conscious as the life literally flowed out of her.

And then Simon had come.

Simon, with his sandy hair and his warm, caring eyes. He had held her hand. She remembered it now. He had asked her to stay with him—prayed over her. He had treated her. She didn't know how he had helped her or what he had done, but she knew that he had been busy.

Everything was so blurry. Another woman. A woman whose tone was sharp rather than warm and gentle. A woman who had hurt her as she massaged Mary's abdomen.

Why would she do that? Had it worked?

Was she dead?

Mary tried to speak again, and this time, she heard voices in the distance—so far away from her.

"She's trying to speak. She's stirring." A male voice was speaking. Simon. He sounded so worried. So fearful. "Mary," he said, and he squeezed her hand. "Mary, squeeze my hand if you can hear me."

She could hear him. But she couldn't squeeze his hand. Even still, she tried, contracting her fingers around his with no idea if she had successfully accomplished the task.

"I felt something," Simon said, and his voice was buoyant now. "Mary! Squeeze again, Mary. We're here. Nora is here. Jessamine is here. The midwife is here. Mary, your daughter is here. We're all waiting for you, Mary."

Her daughter. Simon said her daughter was there. She had a daughter.

Her heart surged with love, and Mary felt a sort of superhuman determination come over her. She tried to open her eyes again, and this time she could feel the lids moving. Light began to filter into her darkness, blinding her with its sudden impact.

"Mary," Simon said. And his face appeared above hers. He looked exhausted, with dark circles beneath his eyes and a thick shadow of a beard along his jaw.

"Simon," she replied, her voice just a whisper. "My daughter."

Something moved beside her, and she felt a weight. Such a small, light weight against her arm. Her head turned, and through her still-blurry vision, she saw the top of her daughter's tiny head.

"Oh," Mary gasped, tears pricking at her eyes. "She's beautiful."

"She's perfect," Nora said, bending down so that she was in Mary's line of vision. "She's been an angel. Breathing well. Strong. She's going to be a little fighter."

Mary was desperate to hold her daughter. She started to move, finding her body still sluggish but more responsive.

"Here," Simon said, helping her to sit up just enough. He propped up pillows behind her and tucked the covers close around her.

Then Nora lifted Mary's daughter into her arms, and for the first time, Mary looked down into her daughter's sweet, red, wrinkled little face. Her heart flipped over in her chest, and she was in love in a way that she had never known was possible. This tiny creature whom she had carried within her for so many months was now here in her arms, living and breathing with a little heart and soul and mind of her own that Mary would watch grow through the years.

"Oh, she's perfect," Mary breathed, happy tears running down her cheeks. "Isn't she beautiful? I've never seen anything so perfect."

Simon sat beside Mary on the bed, and she looked up at him. His eyes were warm, and he reached for her free hand, taking it in his. She couldn't help but smile back at him, knowing without even having to ask that he had come running to save her life—and that he had done it. He had given her this moment.

"She's as beautiful as her mother," Simon told her.

That made Mary realize that she must look quite the mess. For a moment, she worried over it, taking her hand from Simon's to try to smooth down her hair. But then the worry left her as she looked back at her daughter's face, and she didn't care what she looked like or who saw her. This was how a mother looked when she had just brought a life into the world, and Mary would view it as a badge of honor.

"Her name is Grace," Mary murmured, stroking her daughter's cheek. "Grace Victoria Howard." She looked up at Nora and smiled. "Victoria, for Mother."

"She would be pleased," Nora said, smiling through happy tears. "Oh, Mary. You gave us such a scare."

Mary knew she must have, though she didn't remember most of it or what had happened to her. "I'm sorry," she said, looking around the room. "You all look like you have been up for days."

"Don't you apologize," Jessamine said, her voice full of emotion. "All we care about is that you're here, and you and Grace are safe." Jessamine stood from the stool she had been sitting on, motioning to the woman that Mary could only assume was the midwife. "Come on, Martha. Let's fix everyone some much-needed breakfast."

Mary realized that Grace must be hungry as well. "Oh, has she eaten?" Mary asked Nora, alarmed that she might already be failing her little girl.

"We had a wet nurse come by," Nora assured her. "She's down in the room we set up for her, and she's happy to stay as long as she's needed."

"I'm so appreciative," Mary said. "But I would like to feed her myself." She looked at Simon, not sure yet what her condition was. "Is that safe?"

He touched her arm gently. "Not yet. It will be soon. But you have a great deal of medication in you, including pain medications, that would be dangerous for Grace if she were to receive them secondhand through you. We need to give it more time."

She was disappointed, but only for a moment. She was alive, and she would have plenty of time to nurse her daughter. There was no rush right this minute.

Grace stirred in her arms, her little face pinching up even further. One hand reached out, opening and closing as though searching for something. Mary placed her finger against her daughter's palm, and Grace gripped onto it, settling in closer against Mary.

"Oh, what love," Mary whispered. "How can you love something this much so instantly?"

Grace opened her mouth, searching again.

"She's hungry," Mary said, looking up at Nora. "Will you take her to the wet nurse with my thanks?"

"Of course," Nora said, walking over and taking Grace from Mary's arm. Nora kissed Mary's cheek as she straightened back up. "You fought through to come back to us. I'm so glad, Mary. I love you, my sister."

"I love you too," Mary told her as she reluctantly gave Grace up and watched them both walk away.

Suddenly, Mary was alone with Simon. She turned and looked at him, uncertain what she should say. It was clear that he had come running to save her life and that he had worked without rest to make sure that she could live to love and hold her child. She was eternally grateful for his goodness and his protection. He was a man of honor.

But she didn't know where things stood between them. The last conversation they'd had, he had told her that he wanted no relationship with her at all, and she still didn't know what to make of his frequent trips to the saloon or the alcohol scent that lingered around him. She was even less certain about what to do about the fact that despite still not having those answers, she was so glad to see him that she could have jumped into his arms—assuming that her body was capable of it.

"You must have questions," Simon said, reading her mind. "Ask them."

"What happened to me?"

"Would you like the straightforward answer?"

She nodded. "I can handle it."

"You had a postpartum hemorrhage," he said. "They're very dangerous. They often are fatal, in fact."

Mary felt nauseated at the thought. She had known that she had been through something horrible, but having a doctor tell her that her condition was often fatal really brought home the reality of the situation.

"Jessamine came to fetch me when you wouldn't stop losing blood. I gave you medications to try to help, but the truth is that we don't have a good method for stopping a hemorrhage. The medical details as to why aren't important." Simon smoothed the blankets around her, perhaps just so that he would have something to do with his hands. "I stabilized you, and I was about to examine you when Martha arrived. She examined you instead, and she performed abdominal massage and some stitching. It helped, but you weren't recovering yet. We tried to keep you comfortable. The truth is, we prayed over you all night. Between our prayers and the blood transfusions, we kept you with us." His voice wavered faintly. "Thank God."

"You saved my life," Mary said, watching his face. "Thank you, Simon."

"God had mercy on you," Simon replied. "In these situations, there is only so much a doctor can do. I did all of those things, and then I asked God to heal you."

"Why?" Mary asked, the word catching in her throat.

He looked at her, puzzled. "What do you mean why?"

"After our last conversation..."

"Mary," he said, cutting her off. "Even if we had an argument, there is nothing that would stop me from giving everything that I had to keep you here with me. With Grace and Nora and Jessamine." He shook his head at her, as though disappointed that she would ever think otherwise. "I would do it for any patient. But especially for you."

Mary lowered her eyes, a tear slipping down one cheek. "Simon, I don't deserve your kindness."

"Yes, you do."

She shook her head. "I don't. I haven't been honest with you. Not entirely. My husband...Alfred—"

"I know."

Mary looked up at him, confused. "You know?"

"Jessamine told me, on our way here when she brought me to help you," Simon said. "She told me about Alfred and what his drinking had done to you and your marriage and how it had cost him his life."

"Oh." Mary looked down again. "I'm glad that you know. But I'm ashamed that you know as well."

"There's nothing to be ashamed of," Simon insisted, reaching out and tipping her chin up so that she had to look at him. "I wish you had just talked to me, Mary. I wouldn't have held anything against you. I know what it's like to live in fear, second-guessing yourself."

Mary looked into Simon's eyes, and she knew that there was a good man looking back at her. She knew it in a way that she had never known it with Alfred. Even though she had allowed herself to believe that Alfred was good despite his flaws, she had always been forcing that assumption. Now, looking at Simon, it was so different.

"I made so many excuses for Alfred," Mary said quietly. "I kept trusting him and trusting him when I had no reason to, and it...it caused me to doubt myself. My judgment. So I refused to let myself think about all the good in you because it meant I was just doing the same thing again—excusing the warning signs."

He nodded. "I understand that now. And there's something I have to tell you."

She looked back at him, not knowing what to expect. Her fuzzy mind and her exhausted body couldn't take much more shock at this point. But she nodded, asking him to continue.

"Mary, I don't drink."

She frowned. "But..."

He held up a hand, stopping her. "I took a drink once when I was much younger, and I hated it. It seemed like something that I might want to try—just to be rebellious. Adventurous. But it made me sick, and I didn't like the taste or anything else about it. I've never touched a drop since, and I have no desire to."

Stunned, Mary opened her mouth to speak, then closed it, unsure what to say. She didn't want to call him a liar, but she knew what she had seen. She had watched him walk out of the saloon over and over again. She had smelled alcohol on him.

"I know you saw me going in and out of the saloon frequently," Simon said, again reading her mind. "Stan

Bishop runs the saloon, and he's a patient who requires frequent treatments. He doesn't want everyone knowing about his treatments, so I go there to see him. It's more discreet." He gave her a wry smile. "Or at least...it was more discreet until you noticed."

"You're going there to treat a patient?" Mary asked, wanting to make sure that she was hearing what she thought she was hearing. "You're not going there to drink?"

"Not a drop."

"But you smelled like alcohol," Mary said. "I could smell it on you so strongly that day. When I pulled away from you."

Simon looked puzzled for a moment, then he chuckled. "Oh. Stan sometimes has balance issues as part of his condition. He had knocked over a bottle and I had helped him clean it up. Maybe some of it was still on me."

Mary blinked at him in disbelief. All of this time, it had never once occurred to her that Simon would have an alternative explanation for why he had been in the saloon and why he had smelled like alcohol. She had always assumed that his insistence that he wasn't a drunk was based solely on his assessment that he didn't drink to excess—that he had his drinking under control.

But he didn't drink at all. And he had been going to the saloon as an act of service to someone else.

She felt like a fool, and she groaned, covering her face with her hands.

"Mary," Simon said, taking her wrist and tugging her hands away from her face. "Don't."

"I'm a foolish woman," Mary said, staring at him with such remorse that even she knew it was written all over her face. "I cannot tell you how sorry I am, Simon. I judged you so harshly. That's not my nature. I promise it isn't. I don't know what came over me."

He smiled, keeping her hand in his. "We all bring our pasts with us. It's only months ago that you lost your husband because of his struggle with alcohol. You were viewing me through the lens you used to view him."

She nodded. "I was. And you're being very gracious about it, but that does not mean that I am not terribly, terribly sorry."

"You're forgiven," he said simply. But then his face clouded over. "There is something I haven't been honest with you about either."

"What?"

He sighed, looking down at their joined hands. "I don't know if now is the right time to talk to you about this. You have just been through so much, Mary. You're very strong, and you're looking so much better than you have been. But there is no need to add more to your load right now. You should rest and be with your daughter. There will be much time for us to talk in the future."

Mary was about to protest, but Jessamine came walking back in with trays of food, and Mary's stomach betrayed just how hungry she was. Before she knew what was happening, Simon moved from the bed, and Jessamine was setting the tray down. Warm bread smelled fragrant, and eggs from the chicken coop behind the house glistened temptingly. Her stomach growled, and Mary picked up her fork and knife, cutting herself a generous bite.

"After you eat, I need to examine you again," the midwife said, standing by the foot of the bed. "You're looking quite well, but we need to make sure that everything is healing well."

Mary nodded, continuing to eat. A moment later, Nora brought Grace back in, and Mary lit up, setting her breakfast aside and reaching for her daughter. Grace was alert and blinking up at Mary, and Mary couldn't take her eyes off her little girl. Everything else just faded away.

# CHAPTER 10

Simon O'Toole

AUGUST 16, 1888

SIMON KNOCKED ON THE BOARDING HOUSE DOOR, trying to keep under the awning to stay out of the summer storm that was pouring down on him. It wasn't the right day to be traveling about, but it had been two days since he had seen Mary. So many things had been left unsaid between them that morning after the night they weren't sure she would wake up from. But she had pulled through, and they had cleared the air about her mistake about him.

But there was so much more. She had talked to him like a woman who understood how he felt about her...

like a woman who might feel the same way about him.

Nothing like that had been said, though, and he hadn't told her his own secret. Or even his feelings for her, though she had to know from the way he had looked at her, the way he had held her hand in his.

He didn't expect her to be ready to discuss anything then, or maybe even now, given what she had been through and her brand new little girl. But he couldn't wait to see her any longer. She was all he had thought about for two days, and he was surer than ever, after much prayer and consideration, that Mary had come into his world to change his life.

And he needed to know where he stood.

"Simon," Jessamine said, opening the door with a smile. "Come in. You don't have to knock. You know that."

"Well, you never know what might be happening here these days," Simon said with a smile, stepping inside and taking off his hat, shaking the water from it. "I didn't want to intrude. Am I?"

"Not at all," Jessamine assured him. "We always have time for the man who saved my best friend's life."

"How is she?"

"Stronger every day," Jessamine said. "And Grace is precious. She's just a little ray of sunshine every moment of the day."

Simon smiled, remembering the baby's sweet little face and her tiny cry. "I'm sure she is. Is Mary up for visitors?"

"She's right in here," Jessamine said, leading him to the west sitting room. She knocked and poked her head in. "Mary? Simon is here."

"Wonderful. Send him in."

Simon walked into the west sitting room and stopped short, seeing Mary sitting in one of the many chairs, her skirts fanned out around her, her hair swept back from her face, her skin clear and bright, and her eyes filled with love for the little bundle in her arms.

"Mary," he said, swallowing hard at the thought of her two days ago, feverish, limp, and barely holding on. "You look lovely."

"Thank you," she said, smiling. "Come in, Simon. I'm glad you came by."

He walked in and sat down across from her, leaning in to see Grace's sleeping face. "She's just as lovely," he said, feeling an urge to hold the baby that he hadn't expected. But he didn't presume. "How is she?"

"She's doing very well," Mary said. "And so am I. Thanks to you, Simon. Did I properly thank you that day? It's all a blur."

"You did," he assured her. "But it wouldn't have mattered if you hadn't. It was my pleasure."

She smiled warmly at him. "More than I deserve from you, but we won't hash that all over again. I'm glad we've put it behind us, and I hope I didn't make too much trouble for you."

"It's water under the bridge," he said. "But I did come here to talk. If you're willing."

"Of course. I've been wondering a great deal about what you might have wanted to tell me."

He chuckled faintly, rubbing a hand over his face. "Something that I don't often talk about. Frankly, something that is not appropriate for me to talk about with you."

"All right..." Mary said curiously. "I'm listening."

Simon took a deep breath. "Right. You might have noticed that I have never married."

"It occurred to me."

"That's because I cannot have children," Simon said, watching her face. "The details are not important, really. It was an injury as a child. I am a man who cannot give a wife a child."

Mary's brow knit together and she shook her head. "Simon, I'm so sorry. That must be a difficult thing to live with."

"It wasn't," he said. "Because I had committed to never getting married. I didn't want to ever ask a woman to commit to me for life and give up her chance of becoming a mother."

"That's a noble thought," Mary said slowly. "But wouldn't that be her choice?"

"Perhaps," he agreed. "But there are two reasons to marry. One, for convenience. A partnership that mutually benefits both people. And I have little to offer a woman other than stability, and I wouldn't want to hold her need for stability over her head and cause her to give up her chance at children. The second is for love...and love can be a coercive thing. A woman might fall in love and think that she is willing to give up everything only to find out later that she regrets that choice."

Mary nodded, considering his words as she rocked her child. "I suppose the real question is...why are you telling me all of this?"

"Because I love you."

He had expected the words to have an impact, but he still was taken aback by how shocked Mary looked. Surely she must have known. Surely he had been open enough in his actions that his profession wouldn't stun her into stillness, her mouth dropping open.

"Simon..."

"I see I've sprung this on you," he said, trying to keep his voice level and normal. "Obviously I was mistaken in thinking you must know how I felt."

"Simon, wait," Mary said as he started to stand. "Please. Sit. I—you did surprise me, but not in a bad way. Please."

He sat back down, hat in his hands, heart on his sleeve. And he waited for her to speak.

"I didn't know how you felt," Mary said quietly, after a moment of silence. "I didn't let myself believe it. I've been making excuses to myself—other reasons that you might be treating me with such kindness."

"Why?"

"Because I don't deserve you," Mary said, looking at him sadly. "And I'm not the kind of woman who should stand by you as your wife."

Now he was the one who was shocked. "Why would you say that?"

"Because I've made so many mistakes," Mary said. "With Alfred. Marrying him, and then not being able to help him. I just ignored so many things. And moving out here, already with child. Judging you when you were nothing but kind to me. Getting on the bad side of the founding families' daughters. I have not presented myself as...desirable."

"You're wrong," he said, looking into her eyes. "From the moment I saw you, you were desirable to me."

"I was with child."

"It wasn't about that," he said. "It was about who you were. Your spirit. Your gentleness. Your good heart."

"But I was cruel to you."

"You jumped to a conclusion because of a terrible thing that happened to you," Simon said. "I've forgiven you for that, Mary. You have to forgive yourself."

She looked down into Grace's sleeping face, rocking her gently. "Perhaps you're right. What about Grace?"

"I'm sure she forgives you as well."

Mary looked up at him, confused, and he smiled to show that he was joking. She smiled, too, shaking her head at him.

"I mean...she comes with me. As a package deal."

"I know," Simon agreed, his heart swelling as he realized she was contemplating them being together. "I love her too. I could never give you more, but we would always have her."

"I can't have more," Mary whispered, stroking her daughter's cheek. "Martha told me. After she checked on me yesterday."

"Oh, Mary," Simon said, getting up and walking over to her. He knelt by her chair, taking her hand in his.

She squeezed his fingers, looking down into his face. "It's all right, Simon. I would love to have a dozen sweet babies like Grace, but she will be all the more precious to me because she is my only one. I trust in God's plan, and I am so grateful He let me stay here with her."

"Mary," Simon murmured, loving her more with every second. "If you give me a chance, I promise that I will show you how to love me. I love you with all my heart. Enough to take the risk I never thought I would take with any woman. And even if you don't love me now, you can grow to love me; I would give you time. As much as you wanted or needed. I would earn your love."

Mary took her hand from his, and he felt as though his heart had been ripped out of his chest.

But then she laid her finger against his lips, smiling so sweetly at him. "My Simon," she whispered. "I have loved you all this time."

"You have?"

"Of course. Why do you think it hurt me so much when I thought the worst of you?" Mary asked, sweeping his hair back from his forehead. "I thought that I could only choose men who ran to drink. I thought that you had broken my heart."

"I would never," Simon promised, clasping her hand in his and kissing her fingers.

Mary rose, laying Grace down in her little bassinet by the window. Then she walked back over to him, her hands reaching for his as she drew him to stand beside her. "I was determined not to take another husband," she said, laughing at herself. "I was so convinced that my child—my son—and I would live on our own, making our own way in the world. Instead, I got the most wonderful daughter. And I found you."

"And I found you," he said, cupping her face in his hands and looking down into her shining eyes. "Mary."

"Simon," she replied, beaming at him.

He released her and got down on one knee, holding her hand in his as he looked up at her beautiful face. "Mary Howard, I love you with all of my heart, and I will honor and cherish and care for you for the rest of our lives if you will do me the honor of becoming my wife. Will you marry me?"

A tear slid down Mary's cheek, but she was smiling. And then she was laughing with joy. "Yes," she said, nodding. "Simon—yes. Nothing would make me happier."

He stood, and he took her in his arms, holding her close to his chest in a fierce and protective embrace. Just days ago, he had almost lost her, but now she was standing here, her arms around him, agreeing to be his wife. It was a blessing like he hadn't known existed.

"I love you," he said, leaning back just enough to look into her eyes. He cupped her cheek and drew her in, tenderly placing his lips against hers. She leaned into the kiss, and Simon brushed his lips back and forth over hers, enjoying the sweet perfection of the moment.

But it only lasted a moment.

The door to the sitting room flew open, and Jessamine and Nora burst into the room, both of them clapping their hands and then hugging Simon and Mary—much more carefully with Mary than with Simon.

"We are so thrilled," Jessamine said, her hands clasped beneath her chin. "Oh, I was hoping this was what you were here for, Simon. I have to admit that I doubted you when you stayed away for two days. I thought you might be foolish enough to let Mary's mistake fester in your mind again. But you came!"

"I was only staying away to give Mary time to recover," Simon said with a laugh, his arm around his future wife's waist. "She had been through enough without having to endure me stumbling over a proposal."

"It was a lovely proposal," Nora assured him. "Just beautiful."

"Oh, so you were listening," Mary asked with a laugh. "So much for privacy here."

Nora lifted a shoulder, unapologetic in every way. "We're family. There was no way we were going to wait politely in the kitchen."

Grace let out a tiny wail, clearly unhappy that she was not the center of attention at the moment, and Simon stopped Mary from going to her. "Let me," he suggested. "After all, she is part of the package deal I just made. I should bond with her."

Mary beamed up at him. "By all means."

Simon walked over to the bassinet and he picked Grace up, looking at her scrunched-up face and her tiny red fists poking out of the sleeves of her ivory dress. She looked like Mary already, with her dark hair and eyes as blue as the sky. She was a beautiful baby, and as she looked up at him with watering eyes, his heart skipped a beat for her too.

"Shhh," he soothed, bouncing her lightly as he put her up against his shoulder and patted her back. "It's all right, Grace. I'm right here. There you go."

Her cries diminished to whimpers, and he walked Grace back over to the women, smiling with his accomplishment.

"That wasn't so hard," he said, listening to the sound of Grace sniffling herself back to sleep.

Mary chuckled, raising an eyebrow at him. "Wait until she gets serious about it. That was just a tiny protest. She has a good set of lungs, and she can certainly wail when she has a mind to."

"I'll be ready," he promised, using his free arm to put around his new fiancée. "Nothing will keep me from taking care of my two girls."

Mary looked over at Nora but said nothing, and Simon wondered for a minute what the look meant. But then he realized. Of course—Mary had come to Cripple Creek with Nora, and now he was asking her to leave her sister behind.

"Nora, I hope you know that you'll be welcome to move with Mary after we get married," Simon said. "My home is your home as well."

Nora smiled gratefully, but she locked arms with Jessamine and shook her head. "I appreciate the offer, but Jessamine and I have a good system here with the boarding house, and I think I will stay with her and see what we can accomplish." Nora turned her gaze to Mary, fondness in her eyes. "Mary, you needed me when you lived with Alfred, because you needed an ally. But you're marrying a good man this time, and while I'll miss spending every minute with Grace... the three of you will be starting a family. I just hope we get invited over to dinner."

"Any night of the week," Mary promised. She looked up at him, and Simon could tell that she was content with that answer. And if she was content, then so was he. This was just the start of a new life with Mary, where her heart was joined to his. He couldn't wait.

# CHAPTER 11

Mary Howard

IT WAS HER WEDDING DAY. MARY COULD HARDLY believe it. Just a month earlier she would have told anyone who asked that she would never marry again, and that she would spend her life dedicated to raising her son and trust that he would take care of her when he was old enough.

Now, just a few short weeks after moving to Cripple Creek, she had the most beautiful baby girl in the world, and she was marrying the town doctor who had sworn he would never marry. And somewhere in between, she had almost lost her life. It was amazing the twists and turns that God had in store for her, and Mary was learning that she should anticipate each one with joy, because even if it felt terrifying in the moment, later it would lead to some new blessing.

Mary slipped on the dress that she and Nora had worked furiously to make during the past week as they prepared for the wedding. She couldn't hook it up in the back, but Nora would be in momentarily to help her with that. In the meantime, Mary picked Grace up from her bassinet, smiling as the little girl yawned and burbled.

Being a mother had already brought her more joy than she could ever deserve. She kissed Grace's little cheeks and sat down with her, laying Grace on her lap and playing with her tiny hands.

"You are the sweetest thing," Mary murmured to her daughter. "And today you are getting a brand-new daddy. He loves you and he loves your mother and he is going to give us the best life, my little Grace Victoria."

Grace blinked up at her, pursing her lips.

"Are you doubting me?" Mary asked, teasing the little girl with a tap against her upturned nose.

Grace scrunched her nose, then pursed her lips again, making Mary laugh.

"Oh, you're already dressed," Nora said, walking in with two cups of tea in her hand. She set them on the small table to the left of the bedroom door. "Stand up. Let me see you."

With Grace in her arms, Mary stood up, showing off the beautiful ivory dress with its tight bodice and full skirt.

"You look beautiful," Nora said, her voice filled with emotion. "I've never seen a more beautiful bride."

"I can't believe I'm a bride at all," Mary said with a laugh.

"I knew a man would snatch you up," Nora said, moving behind Mary to hook the laces at the back of her dress. "You, my dear sister, are wife material. Any man in his right mind can see that."

"I just hope that I am a better wife this time," Mary murmured. "The more time that passes, the more I blame myself for not forcing Alfred to get help.

Nora turned Mary around, shaking her head firmly. "Enough of that. Enough of Alfred. The man had his good traits, but he was selfish, and he put his own desires before you and your family. Before his faith. It cost him his life, but it didn't cost you yours. Today you start a new life with a man who deserves you and baby Grace."

"I know," Mary said, smiling as she thought of Simon. "And I simply cannot wait."

"Then let's get you ready," Nora urged, sitting Mary down so that she could finish her hair. Nora worked quickly to twist Mary's dark curls up into an elegant up-do, and then she placed the veil at the crown of Mary's head, letting it flow down her back and cover her face.

"You're ready," Nora said, taking Grace from Mary's arms so that Mary could stand and twirl in her dress, her cheeks flushed with happiness and excitement.

Mary nodded, smoothing down her skirts. "I'm ready."

Jessamine came into the room, and the two women hugged. Then Jessamine took Mary's arm and walked her out of the bedroom and down the stairs to the west sitting room in the boarding house, where the pastor, Simon, and their friends waited.

They stopped at the door, and Jessamine hugged Mary again before letting her walk down to Simon on her own.

As Mary walked to meet her soon-to-be husband, she smiled at those who had come to join them on their day. Annie and Jack Lawrence were there, and Annie was beaming at Mary. Beth and Nelly were there as well, much to Mary's surprise. Simon had told her that both women had approached him and apologized for being overly curious about her when she had first arrived and assuming the worst. Mary didn't hold it against them, and she hoped that they could become friends of sorts, even if Mary was sure that she and Beth and Nelly would never be close the way that she and Nora and Jessamine were close. Even still, she had forgiven the women for their meddling ways, and she had gained a great deal of sympathy for Beth, whom Simon had told her was going through a terrible time and refused to get help.

Mary passed by these friends quickly, and then her eyes moved to Simon. The man she was about to marry. He was wearing a suit, and he looked more dashing than ever with his sandy hair slicked back and his face freshly shaven. His eyes were fixed on her, and the look on his face was one of pure love.

It moved Mary, and she smiled, feeling the way that her smile lit up her face. As she reached him, she held her hands out, and he took them in his, drawing her close to him.

"Mary, you look beautiful," he whispered, just to her, the words a secret between them.

Mary pressed his fingers tenderly. "You look so handsome."

"No one will be looking at me," he promised her, drawing her up in front of the pastor, keeping her hands in his.

The pastor began to speak. He talked of God and of love and of the meaning of the marriage bond. As Mary looked into Simon's eyes, she listened to the words, taking in what they meant for her life.

"God has created the marriage bond between a man and a woman," the pastor said. "It is a blessing. An obligation. A partnership. A commitment. When a man and a woman choose to join themselves together, they do so in front of God for a lifetime, and their love for each other is surpassed only by God's love for each of them. There will be good days and there will be bad days. Trials and blessings. Sorrows and joys. Health and illness."

Simon pressed her hands, and she knew what he was telling her. In the short time they had known each other, they had faced all of those things already, and they had come out on the other side. Together.

"No matter what you each face, from this day forward, you will face it as two people who are part of one union," the pastor continued. "Simon, it will be your duty to care for, love, respect, cherish, support, and guide Mary. Mary, it will be your job to care for, love, respect, cherish, support, and guide Simon. Together you will grow your family, and it will be an honor before God. What God has joined together, let no man put asunder."

Mary smiled at Simon, and he grinned back at her.

"Simon, do you take this woman, Mary, to be your lawfully wedded wife?"

"I do," Simon said, without a moment of hesitation.

"Mary, do you take Simon to be your lawfully wedding husband?"

"I do," Mary murmured, happiness blooming within her.

"Then, Simon, repeat after me," the pastor said.

Mary and Simon exchanged their vows, both pledging their hearts and their lives and their faithfulness to each other. And then, finally, the pastor closed his Bible and looked between them.

"Mary and Simon, before God and before these witnesses here today, I join you as man and wife. You are married before God and men."

Simon didn't hesitate. He pulled Mary to him and he kissed her tenderly, his hands framing her face as he held her to him. Mary's stomach fluttered like it did every time he touched her, and she leaned into his kiss as their audience clapped.

It was their first kiss as husband and wife, and it was sweeter than any other Mary had ever had. But they were not alone, and Grace took the liberty of reminding them of that as she let out a wail in Nora's arms, her little fists flailing.

Everyone laughed, including Mary, and she gently eased back from her new husband, touching his cheek tenderly before hurrying over to her daughter and taking her from Nora's arms. She rocked Grace, speaking to her softly, and the little girl settled back down, nestling against Mary and closing her little eyes.

Mary turned to the gathered crowd, bouncing Grace lightly to keep her settled. "Thank you all for being here today with us," she said. "Simon and Grace and I couldn't be happier to share this celebration with you. If you will all make your way to the dining hall, there will be food and fellowship."

Their friends stood, and many stopped to hug her on the way out, congratulating her on the baby and the wedding. Simon hung back, and Mary did as well, walking over to him once they were alone.

She smiled up at him, her eyes twinkling. "Hello, husband."

"Hello, wife," he said, drawing her close for another kiss. "Mary O'Toole."

"Mary O'Toole," she repeated, loving the sound of her new name. "And Grace O'Toole?"

"Really?" he asked, pleasantly surprised. "I wasn't sure if you would want to give her that name."

"Of course I do," Mary said, shaking her head at him. "She's ours, Simon. Mine and yours. Without you, I wouldn't even be here to be her mother. You are and always will be her father."

"We'll have to tell her, of course," Simon said. "I don't want her to be deceived."

"Of course," Mary agreed. "She will always know that you chose her and that you wanted both of us. That you are her father because you loved her. Not just that you love her because you are her father."

Simon stared at her, awe in his eyes. "I love you, Mary O'Toole. You are the best thing that has ever happened to me."

"I love you, too," she said. Then, with a wink, she added, "And you are the second best thing that has ever happened to me."

He laughed, looking down at Grace. "I can accept that. Who could look at her little face and not think she is the most wonderful thing in the world?"

"Not me," Mary said, kissing Grace's forehead. "Come. We need to entertain our guests. Then we can go home."

Together, they walked into the dining hall. Simon went to thank the pastor and get them some food, and Mary found herself standing with Beth Brown and Nelly Johnson.

"Mary," Nelly said, reaching out to touch Mary's arm. "Beth and I have been talking, and we want you to know how truly sorry we are about everything that happened when you first arrived. We were being foolish. It was not becoming of us."

Mary had long since let that go, but she was curious. "Why did you approach me that day and lie about Eliza Mason?" she asked. "What did you want?"

Beth shook her head. "We had no good reason. We saw you get off the train and it was clear there was no man with you. We...were being meddlesome, and we wanted some excuse to find out who you were and what your story was."

"Why not just ask me?"

"Believe it or not, we thought that would be unmannerly," Nelly said.

The three women laughed, Beth and Nelly more awkwardly than Mary.

"It sounds so foolish," Beth said, shaking her head. "You know, Simon told me the other day that I've become quite the gossip, and I suppose that he's right. Nelly and I have talked, and we're going to try to have purer intentions. The truth is, we sometimes get bored, I suppose. Or frustrated with our own lives. And the excitement of figuring out if there is a scandal afoot..."

"I understand," Mary said, not making Beth drag out the explanation any further when Beth was clearly feeling guilty. "We all make mistakes. I am first in line to admit that. I'm just glad that we have things sorted out between us now."

Beth nodded. "We mean to make things right with Jessamine too. I'm sure she's told you that she is not very fond of us."

"Well, you did question her ability to run the boarding house," Mary pointed out, bouncing Grace lightly as the little girl burbled in her sleep.

"Like Beth said, we're changing our ways," Nelly said. "We've realized that the things we say actually can hurt people."

"I've learned that lesson too," Mary said. "There's no hard feelings between us, ladies, and I hope that we can be friends. I'm sure that if you speak honestly with Jessamine, she'll let the past go too. Jessamine has a big heart."

Beth nodded, and because they were being open, Mary decided to pose the question.

"Beth, is everything all right at home?"

With a sigh, Beth looked down at her hands and then out the window for a moment before facing Mary again. "Truthfully? No, it is not. I've been trying to put on a brave face, but it seems everyone knows anyway. My husband, James. Things were strained between us for a while, and one day...almost a year ago now...he left on a trip to buy supplies. He's never returned."

Mary knew what it took for Beth to admit that, and her heart went out to the woman. "Beth, I'm sorry," she said. "I know that must be very difficult for you. Have you heard from him at all?"

"No," Beth said, shaking her head. "But he keeps in touch with his parents sometimes, so we know he is alive. He just...doesn't want to come home."

Mary shifted Grace so that she could hold her with one arm, then reached her hand out and took Beth's, pressing gently. "You know, my first husband...his name was Alfred. He had a terrible drinking problem, and it was very difficult to live with him sometimes. I made a lot of excuses and blamed myself for his failures, but the truth was that it was Alfred making the bad decisions. Not me. And if James has abandoned his family, that's his bad decision. It's not your fault."

"I may be hard to live with," Beth said, still looking down.

"I don't know if you are or not," Mary said honestly. "But I know that a man of honor—a man of God— doesn't abandon his family even if there is something difficult. You have a good heart, Beth, or you wouldn't have apologized to me. If your husband doesn't want to see that and work together with you, then that's his fault."

Beth gave her a grateful smile, but she didn't say anything.

"That's what I've told her," Nelly agreed. "James has always had a wild nature. He just doesn't like to be stuck in one place. He's always here, there, and every-where. I still think he'll come back and things will go back to normal."

Mary watched Beth, wondering if that was even possible after a year apart. "Is that what you want, Beth?"

"I want my family back," Beth said. "I have always loved James. I always will. I'm just not sure he can ever love me the same way."

"I'll pray that he has a change of heart," Mary said as Simon joined them, plates of food in hand.

"Thank you, Mary," Beth said sincerely. "But you shouldn't spend any more of your wedding day worrying over me. I'm just fine."

"How's little Harry?" Simon asked. "Is his arm still healing?"

"It is, and he's proud of his battle wounds," Beth said with a smile. "Thank you for asking."

"I'll be out this week to check on him," Simon promised before leading Mary to sit down at the table so that they could enjoy their wedding meal with everyone.

Mary sat with Grace on her lap, Simon on her left and Nora on her right. Jessamine sat across from her, and Annie and Jack were nearby. Beth and Nelly sat down on Simon's other side, and the other guests joined them around the table, all talking and laughing.

Mary ate the food that Annie had so generously agreed to provide for their celebration, and she looked around at her new life, amazed at how much she had been blessed. Cripple Creek was never in her plan, but here she was, married to the town doctor, with a beautiful baby in her arms, with friends and family that were better than any other. And Annie's fresh apple pie waiting to be sliced into for dessert. Tonight, she and Simon would sleep in her new home together. And tomorrow would be the first full day of the best life that she could have ever been given. She was Mary O'Toole of Cripple Creek, Colorado, and by God's great mercy, she was home.

# EPILOGUE

Delia Mahogany

Rain fell in torrents all around her, but that didn't slow down Delia Mahogany. She was no stranger to the elements, and a bit of rain didn't bother her one bit, even if she was riding in an open buggy, with no protection, along the dusty roads that led to Cripple Creek, Colorado. Her dark hair, which was swept back off her face in an up-do that barely contained the wild corkscrew curls that always threatened to break free, was drenched with rainwater, and rivulets rolled down the back of her neck, seeping into the white collar of her dress. She didn't mind. It kept her nice and cool on an unusually steamy Colorado day.

Besides, there were far more important things on her mind than the weather. She was on her way to Cripple Creek because she was moving there to become the new schoolteacher for the year. It was her first teaching job, and she was filled with nervous excitement and a determination to succeed.

Delia had grown up in Ralston, Colorado, about two hours from Cripple Creek on horseback. Until that very morning, she had lived there with her mother and father, helping her mother run the farmhouse while her father worked in the fields. But Delia had always known that she wanted more than her mother's life—and not because she looked down on her mother. In fact, she thought her mother was one of the best people in the world, with her gentle, patient spirit and her loving hands that baked bread and cleaned and sewed and washed all day long.

But Delia had never been like her mother. She was never content to stay at home—always wanted to be out in the world, seeking new adventures and taking on new challenges. That was why she had gotten in trouble so many times during her teenage years for sneaking out to the stables, where she would take care of the horses and go riding with the stable hands. She felt freest when she was riding, much to her parents' chagrin. They both agreed that Delia should adopt more genteel ways. But Delia was now twenty years old, and people were finally beginning to realize that she wasn't going to change.

That didn't mean that her parents had been happy when Delia had announced that she was taking the Cripple Creek teaching job, though. Neither of them wanted her off on her own, living in the little house that came with the job, on her own for the first time. Delia had spent many evenings talking with her parents, convincing them that she was not dishonoring herself or them by moving away without a husband and settling in some new town.

In the end, she had never convinced them, but they had not tried to stop her from going. And now she was on her way, ready to start the new chapter of her life that would bring...anything.

"We're almost there, miss," the driver said, turning back to look at her, the rain running off his hat in streams. "Not much longer now."

"Don't worry about me," Delia called back. "I'm enjoying the trip very much."

He looked curious, but he said nothing, turning back to look at the road ahead.

In mere moments, Delia could see the first buildings on the outskirts of Cripple Creek. Houses at first, and several stables from what she could tell. Then, as they passed those, they entered the heart of the town, where a row of shops and other buildings sat on either side of a main street that was completely empty of people.

The driver stopped, looking around. "Isn't someone meeting you, miss?"

"I'm sure they're around here somewhere," Delia said, picking up her case and standing. "I can wait. There's no need for you to stay. I appreciate you driving me out here in the rain." She reached into her satchel and pulled out the coins that she had saved for his payment.

He accepted them gratefully, nodding to her. "I don't like leaving you alone, miss. With the weather this way, there might be no one to meet you, and you'll be stranded. There's a boarding house nearby. I can take you there."

"Oh, I'm sure someone will be out to meet me. They know I'm coming," she said, climbing down from the coach, case in one hand and satchel over her shoulder. "I sent them a letter."

The driver looked dubious, but he had delivered her, and he had been paid. His job was done. He tipped his hat to her and sat back down on his seat, snapping the reins so that the horses took off again. And just like that, he drove away and back out of town.

Delia looked around her. It was true that there really wasn't a single person in sight, but she still didn't find that too unusual. She had told the town board members that she would arrive this afternoon, but she hadn't been able to give them a specific time given that the journey could involve any number of delays.

She would simply walk around until she ran into someone who could point her in the right direction. The rain was growing lighter anyway, and soon enough it would clear. She liked the look of the town in the rain. It gave Cripple Creek an almost romantic look, the white buildings standing out starkly beneath the gray sky and the falling rain. Puddles gathered in the streets, begging for children to splash through them with their siblings, drawing the affectionate ire of their mother.

There was a little restaurant up ahead, and Delia walked toward it, certain that she would find someone within who could help her get settled.

And, sure enough, when Delia walked in, she found two women sitting at a table. One was older and one was younger, but both smiled at her when they saw her, then quickly got to their feet, clearly concerned with her rather sodden appearance.

"Oh, look at you," the younger woman said. "You've been caught in this terrible downpour."

"I don't mind it," Delia assured her. "It's just a little rain. I came in hoping that someone could point me toward Matthew Brown or Elliott Wilson. I'm Delia Mahogany, the new schoolmistress, and I'm supposed to meet them today for a tour of the town and my new living space."

"Oh, I see," the young woman said. "I'm not sure you'll find them in town today. They're both on the town board, and I believe the town board members are away today. In a meeting with a neighboring town about an issue with tainted water." She turned toward the older woman. "Is that right, Annie?"

"Yes," Annie confirmed. "My Jack is with them. I'm afraid they plan to be away all day."

For the first time, Delia felt a bit put out. "I see," she said. "Did this just come up?"

"Yes, we just learned about the tainted water a day or two ago," the younger woman said. "I'm sure they meant for someone to meet you, and with this crisis on their hands, it just slipped their minds."

Delia sighed, but then she shook it off. There was no sense letting a mishap upset her excitement about starting this new job in this new town. She would simply figure out a solution that would work for her until someone could greet her properly. "Well, no matter," she said. "I heard there's a boarding house in town?"

"Yes," the younger woman said. "My name is Nora West. I work at the boarding house, actually. My dear friend Jessamine owns the place. We'd be happy to put you up for the night."

"How convenient that I should meet you here, then," Delia said with a smile. "Thank you, Nora. I would appreciate the hospitality."

"Of course," Nora said, turning to Annie. "Annie, do you have anything warm on hand? Delia, you must be hungry, I'm sure. Annie is a legendary cook."

Delia put her things down and took a seat at a table. "Actually, I'm famished, yes. Thank you."

"I'll put a plate on for you," Annie said, hurrying off into the kitchen and leaving Delia and Nora on their own.

"So," Nora said, taking a seat across from Delia. "A schoolteacher. That must be very rewarding."

"I don't know," Delia said with a laugh. "This will be my first time. But I imagine it will be rewarding, and I'm quite anxious to get started. Are there many school-age children in town?"

Nora nodded. "Quite a few. The founding families have more grandchildren than you can keep track of."

"The founding families?"

"Yes, the Wilsons, the Lawrences, the Johnsons, and the Browns," Nora told her. "They came here back in the 1860s, and they started this town themselves. They still form the core of its center, and their families have expanded. Beth Brown, for instance, is Elliott Wilson's daughter, and she married James Brown, Matthew Brown's son, and Beth and James have four children together. Nelly Johnson used to be Nelly Lawrence, but she married Wesley Johnson, and they have seven children under nine years old."

Delia's eyes widened. "Oh my. So that's eleven children between two families?"

Nora nodded.

"And there are more?"

"Quite a few more."

"I'm never going to be able to keep them all straight," Delia said with a laugh. "I have no idea who belongs to which family already."

Nora laughed, too, then she took another look at Delia. "You really are soaking. Let me start the fire and get you a towel for your hair."

"That would be lovely," Delia agreed. She wasn't terribly worried about her hair, but she was starting to feel a bit of a chill, and she didn't want to spend her first week in town recovering from a cold.

Nora got up and placed some logs in the fireplace, stoking them and then lighting a match. They caught the flame quickly, and a small fire roared into being, giving off a wave of heat in the room. Then Nora handed Delia some towels from behind the counter of the restaurant, and Delia took her hair down to press the strands between the fabric.

"Are you from Cripple Creek, then?" Delia asked. "You seem to know everyone."

"Actually, I've only been here a little over a month," Nora said. "I moved here with my sister, Mary, to live with Jessamine. Mary has since gotten married to Simon O'Toole. He's the town doctor."

Delia lifted her eyebrows with interest. "What a love story that must have been."

"It was," Nora said with a laugh. "Quite. So now it's just Jessamine and me at the boarding house."

"No love story of your own?"

Nora shook her head. "Hardly. Mary has always been the one that catches a man's eye. She is sweet and delicate and pretty as a flower. Not to mention charming and funny."

"She sounds lovely," Delia agreed. "But you shouldn't sell yourself so short. You're lovely yourself."

"Thank you," Nora said, pleasantly surprised. "As are you."

Delia laughed and gestured to herself. "Well, you haven't caught me looking my best, but thank you all the same."

Annie reappeared, a bowl of warm stew and a cup of coffee in her hands. She set both in front of Delia and then sat down with the two women. Delia took a bite, and her eyes widened.

"That does qualify as legendary," she said sincerely. "Annie, you will have yourself a new customer very shortly. I'm afraid that my mother's domestic skills did not pass down to me the way that we both hoped they would, and this is far better than anything that I could scrape together in the kitchen."

Annie clucked her tongue and shook her head. "Now, now. Anyone can learn skills in the kitchen. It's not magic. It's patience and determination."

"I'm sure that's true," Delia agreed. "And that might explain my downfall. Patience is not my strong suit."

She ate the warm meal eagerly, the fire erasing the cold from the rain. As she did, Annie and Nora proved to be good company, chatting with her about the town and the people and where she had come from. Before Delia knew it, an hour had passed, and as there was still no sign of anyone from the board coming to meet her, she figured that she might as well get settled for the night. The rain had petered off, and Nora was happy to walk her back to the boarding house.

Delia stood, clearing her own plates for Annie and then picking up her bags.

"Annie, it's been a pleasure, and you will absolutely see me again soon."

"I hope to," Annie said. "Come back anytime."

Nora walked Delia outside, and they both walked along the waterlogged streets, Nora pointing out little shops and tidbits about the town as they went. As they walked, Delia looked around her, drinking it all in and deciding that her new home had a great deal of potential.

But then she stopped in her tracks and dropped her bags. Up ahead, a man was yanking on a horse's reins. The horse was shying away from him, tossing his head back and forth, clearly unhappy with being forced to do whatever the man was trying to make the horse do. The man, irate, hit the horse across the face and shouted, waving his arms and yanking so hard on the reins that the bit in the horse's mouth strained against its teeth and lips.

Rage flowed through Delia, and without even thinking, she went storming toward the man, skirts in her hands so that she could move faster down the street. No one treated an animal like that in front of her and got away with it. And she didn't care if she was a newcomer in this town and a woman who most would think had no business speaking her mind.

If this town wanted a schoolteacher who didn't speak her mind, they had hired the wrong woman, and they might as well find that out right now!

**To continue enjoying** Cripple Creek Colorado Gold Series **(12 Book Series) Please go to**

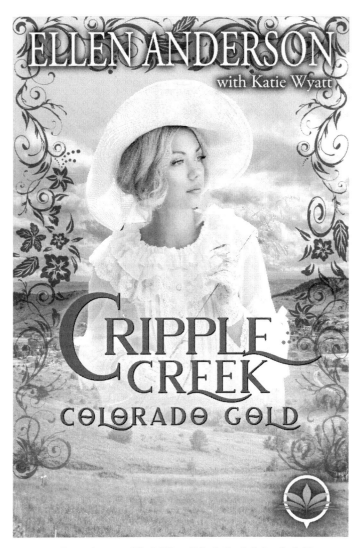

*Ellen Anderson and Katie Wyatt Cripple Creek Colorado Gold Series( 12 Book Series)*

ELLEN ANDERSON & KATIE WYATT

RECOMMENDED READS OTHERS BOOKS STORIES OLD
and new from our library of love

# COMPLETE SERIES
# Sweet Western Romance

KATIE WYATT, BRENDA CLEMMONS AND ELLEN ANDERSON

*Ellen Anderson Katie Wyatt Box Set Mail Order Bride Historical
Western Romance Complete Series*

*Katie Wyatt Mega Box Set Series (12 Mega Box Set Series)*

ROYCE CARDIFF PUBLISHING HOUSE PRESENTS other wonderful clean, wholesome and inspiring romance short stories titles for your entertainment. Many are value boxset and as always FREE to Kindle Unlimited readers.

*Brenda Clemmons Box Set Sweet Clean*
*Contemporary Romance Series*

*Thank you so much for reading our book. We sincerely hope you enjoyed every bit reading it. We had fun creating it and will surely create more.*

*Your positive reviews are very helpful to other reader, it only takes a few moments. They can be left at Amazon.*

*https://www.amazon.com/Ellen-Anderson/e/B07B8C952M*

**Want free books every month? Who doesn't!**

*Become a preferred reader and we'll not only send you free reads, but you'll also receive updates about new releases.*

*So you'll be among the first to dive into our latest new books, full of adventure, heartwarming romances, and characters so real they jump off the page.*

*It's absolutely free and you don't need to do anything at all to qualify except go to.*

**PREFERRED READ FREE READS**

*https://ellenanderson.gr8.com/*

# ABOUT THE AUTHORS

ELLEN ANDERSON STARTED LIFE NEAR SEDONA, Arizona, surrounded by the most beautiful scenery the West has to offer, along with its intricate history and myriad legends. Her favorite memories are of camping out on the family property under the vast canopy of stars, listening to her father and grandfather tell stories.

Eventually, Ellen began writing her own stories, mixing her up-close-and-personal western experiences with special characters who share her unique sense of fun and adventure.

When she met her handsome husband on a horse drive, her path to writing historical western romances was sealed.

Today, Ellen and her husband still do some work on the family ranch, and their children are following in the family tradition, helping care for the Anderson horses. In her spare time, Ellen enjoys photography, swimming, trying out unique historical recipes from scratch and exploring ghost towns in the family RV.

KATIE WYATT IS 25% AMERICAN SIOUX INDIAN. Born and raised in Arizona, she has traveled and camped extensively through California, Arizona, Nevada, Mexico, and New Mexico. Looking at the incredible night sky and the giant Saguaro cacti, she has dreamed of what it would be like to live in the early pioneer times.

Spending time with a relative of the great Wyatt Earp, also named Wyatt Earp, Katie was mesmerized and inspired by the stories he told of bygone times. This historical interest in the old West became the inspiration for her Western romance novels.

Her books are a mixture of actual historical facts and events mixed with action and humor, challenges and adventures. The characters in Katie's clean romance novels draw from her own experiences and are so real that they almost jump off the pages. You feel like you're walking beside them through all the ups and downs of their lives. As the stories unfold, you'll find yourself both laughing and crying. The endings will never fail to leave you feeling warm inside.

Printed in Great Britain
by Amazon

16588129R00130